THE
SAVAGE
LANDS

THE
SAVAGE
LANDS

ANDY BRIGGS

OPEN ROAD
INTEGRATED MEDIA
NEW YORK

Cover design by the-parish.com and Andrea C. Uva

ISBN 978-1-4804-0014-6

Published in 2013 by Open Road Integrated Media, Inc.
345 Hudson Street
New York, NY 10014
www.openroadmedia.com

THE
SAVAGE
LANDS

1

"**A**re you sure?" The jeweler held the gemstone up to the light and pressed his loupe close to it. The muscles around his eye stiffened to hold the lens firmly in place as he studied the gem, admiring the spiraling snake motif delicately carved across the surface.

"I will give you two hundred dollars," he said, laying the stone back onto the black cotton bag it had come in. His face was emotionless, desperate not to betray just how much he wanted it.

Albert Werper's palms became slicker, and not just because of the overbearing humidity of Brazzaville, the capital city of the Republic of the Congo. He stared at the opal. He knew the jeweler was offering him a poor price, but Werper was a terrible haggler and he desperately needed the money. Back in Belgium, he had no need to haggle, and found the concept uncivilized. He nodded. What was two hundred dollars to him? There would be millions where that came from.

Werper quickly left the boutique, the jeweler closing the heavy iron gate behind him, forcing peeling paint to fall from the already dilapidated building. He was shaking so hard with excitement, lost in thoughts of hidden treasure, that he almost walked into the stream of traffic slicing through the street. Motorcycles darted around him, the croaking horns of several trucks making him jump back onto the pavement. He forced himself to focus on not getting himself killed. He found a break in the traffic and jogged across the street. With his starched clothes and sunburn, he stood out from the bustling dark-skinned crowds.

Across the road, he found a café with a couple of plastic tables overlooking a huge, turbid-brown stretch of the Congo River. On the distant bank stood another capital city—Kinshasa, of the Democratic Republic of the Congo, a much less stable country than the one he was in now, and the location of his ultimate goal. Finally, he was close to uncovering the truth he had been obsessively pursuing. He ordered a beer, throwing a few francs to the young girl serving him, then made sure the girl was out of earshot before he dialed a number on his mobile phone. The call was answered on the second ring.

"Well?" said a terse voice.

"Opal," confirmed Werper, unable to keep the thrill out of his voice. "The finest quality. I was right, I was right!" he said excitedly, forgetting to keep his voice down.

"Excellent news, but without the map . . ." the voice of his financier cut in.

Werper's excitement made him feel bold. For too long he had felt bullied by his private financier—an aristocratic English businessman—but now the tables were turning. Werper had become invaluable.

"Then we find it! I was right about the opal. . . . I am right about everything, if only you'd listen!" he slammed his hand on the plastic table, causing his beer to teeter dangerously. He quickly righted it as the frothy amber liquid spilled over his khaki pant leg, and he cursed in French under his breath. "Listen, we're a step closer to the Savage Lands, just like the legend states. And there—"

"This is not a secure line," growled the voice curtly. "Very well. It appears you are right after all."

They spoke for a minute longer, Werper listening to a string of instructions and mentally noting a shopping list of equipment before the line went dead. He tapped the phone on the table with nervous energy. His life's work was about to come to fruition—not bad for a thirty-four-year-old. He would be rich beyond even his own greedy imagination.

. . .

Tarzan was sure the earth trembled. Even the movement of his ape family, the Mangani, would not invoke such a response from the ground, yet Tarzan was certain the ground had shifted beneath his bare feet. Only a fraction, but it unnerved him never-theless—perhaps the passing of some other great beast?

His family was spread across the rolling mountain flank, picking choice roots or lazily pulling bamboo branches down to feed from the prime shoots. It had been a while since the Mangani had fed so well and contentment spread across the band in a series of low satisfied coughs. Even Kerchak, the aging silverback, was relaxed enough to ignore the over-exuberant capering of the young apes led by Karnath. Their playful romps would usually send the old cur-mudgeon into a roaring fit, but not today. Today, all was peaceful.

Yet Tarzan could not shake the feeling that had been grow-ing in the pit of his stomach. He dug his toes into the ground as if they were roots with which he could sense further vibrations. The dirt was unusually warm around his toes, and he closed his eyes to heighten his other senses. Despite the lush foliage, the air was tinged with a foul smell that grew worse and turned his stomach. When the wind changed direction the scent was carried away, but it was still strong enough to be detected. And it masked the scent of possible intruders into their territory.

Tarzan adroitly leaped onto a boulder, which angled from the ground like a ramp, offering a clear view down the grassy incline to the start of the jungle a dozen yards farther down. The lush green-ery rolled to a valley below, rising on the other side to mountain peaks that faded into the morning mist. The ape-man focused, blocking out the sound of the Mangani around him so he could detect the slightest sigh in the trees.

There. An almost imperceptible swish of branches being pulled aside, carefully enough not to snap them, but with enough force to allow something of size to walk by. There was more than one creature out there; Tarzan was sure of it. He was so focused that he flinched when Kerchak appeared just beneath him and grunted. The old ape had picked up on Tarzan's anxiety and followed his gaze to the trees. Despite their frequent disagreements, Tarzan was glad the old silverback was with him. These were dangerous lands, and every tooth and claw counted, even if age and unpleasant vapors had numbed Kerchak's senses.

The hairs on Tarzan's neck rose. A lifetime of survival in the jungle had taught him to rely on his basic instincts. He gave a sharp, gruff bellow from deep in his chest that carried across the gorillas. Instantly they froze, looking around with concern.

For a long time no one moved and nothing stirred in the trees. Tarzan sensed the younger apes were growing restless, so he lightly dropped from the boulder, landing on all fours. Hunched over, copying Kerchak's swagger, he slowly approached the edge of the jungle. Kerchak kept close to the rest of the family. If anything happened to Tarzan, he was the second line of defense.

The looming jungle towered over Tarzan, the canopy so thick he could see nothing but darkness beyond. He stopped just an arm's length from the trees and squinted into the black expanse.

Then he heard it, the faintest rasping of a breath from his left. Before he could turn his head to target the sound, a flock of yellow birds blustered from the trees to his right, startled by the pale-furred figure that leaped down from the tree with a snarling howl.

Targarni. The dwellers of the land Tarzan had led his hungry family to. The powerful chimpanzees ferociously protected their fertile home, and Tarzan had already had several run-ins with the thugs. He raised his arms to shield himself from a sudden attack—a move that left him wide open from the other two apes charging from the side. The impact sent him sprawling onto his back.

The assault was fast and intelligently coordinated, giving Tarzan no time to rise to his feet. The Targarni were nothing more than pale-gray blurs leaping from the trees and sprinting toward the gorillas. Kerchak saw Tarzan fall and gave a bellow that drew six other males from the band forward. They were young apes, their backs just showing signs of turning silver. But what they lacked in experience, they made up for in courage as they charged the Targarni.

Tarzan felt teeth sink into the meat of his thigh, but he bore the pain through gritted teeth. Three chimps leaned their weight on him, but even on his back, Tarzan was a formidable opponent. An elbow smashed into the snout of one Targarni while Tarzan's other hand grabbed the throat of the chimp whose teeth were gnashing close to his face. Tarzan's arm trembled with the effort of holding the ape back, and with a mighty roar he kicked out at the thug who had bit him. His foot caught the Targarni male in the stomach and the ape was catapulted into the air, back into the trees. Tarzan then pulled forward the chimp he still had by the throat and used him as a shield. The third Targarni Tarzan had punched tried to bite him, but instead bit into the back of his companion.

Kerchak led the cavalry charge, sprinting downhill at an astonishing speed. The Targarni quickly retreated to the trees as the line of gorillas bore down on them.

Tarzan struck his bare chest and howled the cry of a bull ape as the cowards vanished into the trees. Once again, Tarzan had thwarted the Targarni's ambush. But he was worried. Their number had been so small—a raiding party rather than a full-fledged attack. A warning to the Mangani gorillas to stay away. As if to emphasise that, Tarzan caught a glimpse of white fur high in the trees. One bloodshot eye peered down at him. The albino ape hissed a warning before vanishing into the jungle. Tarzan had named the white ape—Goyad. The Targarni leader was almost twice the size of his minions and much more intelligent. The Mangani had been warned—but Tarzan was the proud king of all he surveyed. He did not heed warnings, he gave them.

The ground trembled beneath his legs with more force than before, and a low rumble echoed across the jungle sending thousands of birds haphazardly into the air.

Everything was about to change.

2

The earth shuddered and camp Karibu Mji rattled. The illegal logging camp, built deep in the Congolese rainforest, was not designed to withstand such force. Corrugated roofs shook, and timber joints popped nails, some crashing to the floor. Latches jarred loose and doors swung open. From the bar's kitchen, a great clattering of pots and pans were followed by Esmée's anxious cries.

Jane Porter lay in a hammock strung between two lodges. It swayed a little but absorbed the worst of the tremor. She lowered her book and looked around in alarm.

"Esmée?" she called out, dropping from the hammock. The moment her boots touched the ground she could feel the earthquake's pulse. She took a step toward the bar but halted when a massive clatter rose from her left. Human wails cut across the monotonous bass rumble of the shifting earth. Jane changed direction and ran to the edge of the camp.

The northern periphery of the logging camp was used to stack rare hardwood that the loggers had felled but not yet had chance to float downriver. Jane arrived in time to see that the iron stakes used to keep the pyramid of logs in place had twisted in the ground. The fifteen-foot-high stack was crashing downward in a wooden avalanche. Loggers were fleeing the deadly cascade.

Robbie Canler sprinted across the clearing as several tons of lumber chased after him. Jane caught her breath, not daring to shout out his name in case it distracted him. Robbie threw himself behind a bulldozer for cover just as the logs clanged against the side of the machine with enough force to buckle the metal.

One not-so-fortunate logger was lost under the timber, his screams drowned out as he was flattened. Jane quickly looked away. She had witnessed much brutality in the jungle and had no wish to see more. Her heart was pumping, adrenaline surging as she tried to make sense of what was happening around her. She searched for her father, hoping he was safe. Instead, she saw Mr. David, the camp's unofficial manager—a man who had put his own life on the line to search for her when she had once gone missing and was later saved by Tarzan. Mr. David had fallen, his foot caught in a tangle of dense roots poking from the dirt. His eyes were wide in panic, his fingers clawing the soil in an attempt to pull himself away. A log the length of a lorry trailer and width of a child was bearing down on him. On instinct, Jane ran toward him.

The jungle had hardened Jane to the realities of life and death so she didn't dwell on the danger. Her focus was on the narrow margin of survival Mr. David had left. As she reached him, she ignored his flailing hands and his pleas to be pulled out. Instead she ran straight to the roots. The log accelerated toward them. Jane knew she had seconds.

Mr. David's foot was deeply entangled. She tore at the roots, but they were too tough to break. The rushing log was certain to crush them both. She had to decide whether to stay or flee for her own life.

"Jane!" Mr. David howled with fear as Jane pulled away. His first thought was that she had abandoned him—but to his surprise she stooped to retrieve a discarded shovel a few feet away. She hefted it up, the metal beneath the dirt-encrusted blade catching the sun. Jane swung the shovel at Mr. David's leg as hard as she could. He felt nothing but knew she had severed his foot.

A second later Mr. David felt himself pulled aside, but he was too weak to do anything. A huge rush of air and the log jounced past him. Then silence. The quake had ended.

Lying on her back in the dirt, Jane caught her breath. Mr. David was slouched half across her. Her heart was pounding from exertion and she only opened her eyes when Mr. David groaned in pain.

"Thank you," he muttered. "My . . . my foot . . . ?"

Jane grimaced as she looked down at him. "Looks like you're gonna need some new shoes."

Mr. David gathered his courage and followed her gaze. His brown toes wiggled freely in the air. Jane hadn't severed his foot, but hacked his boot open, allowing his foot to slip out. An inch higher and he would have lost the limb. . . . But that didn't matter. He began to laugh, a few rare tears of gratitude rolling down his cheek.

"Help me!" called another voice.

Jane stood and tried to pinpoint the voice. The log that had almost squashed her had crashed through several camp cabins, but they should have been empty. Other logs lay scattered across the clearing like spilt toothpicks. Robbie emerged from behind the bulldozer.

"Help!"

Robbie located the source of the sound and ran toward it. "Over here!" he yelled to Jane.

Several yards away a heavy rosewood tree had slammed into the treeline at the edge of the camp. Two figures were wedged between the log and a pair of thick moabi trees—Jane's father, Archie, and Lord William Greystoke. The English lord had his arm draped around Archie—it was obvious he had been pushing the man to safety ahead of himself. The dense jungle had stopped the wayward log mere inches from crushing them, but had now pinned them against the trees.

Robbie and a pair of Indian loggers tried to free the two men, but the rare hardwood timber was too heavy.

"Get me a chainsaw!" yelled Robbie. Within half a minute the sound of a revving chainsaw tearing into wood echoed through the clearing as the men were cut free.

Clark, the South African who had persuaded Archie to start the logging expedition, limped over on an ornate rosewood walking stick. A leopard had slashed his leg when he'd followed Jane after she had stolen a jeep. The damage to the muscle meant he would never walk properly again. It was a physical wound he was more than happy to remind Jane about constantly.

A search of the area revealed one logger dead and three who had sustained various injuries. The casualties were taken to the camp bar, the most hygienic place in Karibu Mji, for Archie to tend to their wounds. As a trained doctor, he was their best chance, and the camp cook, Esmée, a native Congolese, knew more than enough natural remedies to make herself useful.

It wasn't until night began to fall that the funeral for the dead logger, whose real name nobody knew, was held in a clearing half a mile from camp. He was laid to rest in a dirt grave without even a basic headstone. As Clark had pointed out on many occasions, their presence in the jungle was not legal, and a gravestone was just another way to draw unwanted attention to them.

• • •

That night everybody congregated in the bar to eat warm stew, which Esmée ladled out generously. The atmosphere was subdued. A camp death was considered a bad omen, and they had seen more than their fair share of them when faced with rebel guerrillas and poachers. The earthquake had brought a whole new dimension of despair to the team.

"A damn quake, out 'ere. Who'da thought it?" grumbled Clark as he swilled his half-full bottle of Tusker beer.

"This entire area is tectonically active," said William Greystoke, his Etonian voice sounding out of place in a camp full of hardened law-breaking loggers. He was a privileged Englishman who had recently inherited his father's title of "lord." After Clark contacted him with proof that Greystoke's long-lost cousin was alive and well in the jungle, Greystoke had visited the logging camp to see for himself. "My family has drawn up several geological surveys over the years—for our business interests, you understand. Indeed, that is partly what Uncle John was doing when his plane went down." He cast an eye across the bar toward Robbie and Jane who sat together, refusing to sit with the English lord. They had made their views clear: He was not welcome. Clark and Archie, on the other hand, had greeted him with open arms. Not because they enjoyed his snarky company, but because they planned to claim the reward money offered for reuniting the Greystoke family.

"What kind of business interests?" Clark asked casually.

William smiled. "We have several, but I assure you, with the help you are about to give me, all of this," he gestured around him, "will be conveniently forgotten."

Archie looked at him thoughtfully. He didn't entirely trust Lord Greystoke, but the man *had* just saved his life. . . .

"So you still want to find your cousin?"

"I would not be here if that were not the case," said Greystoke with a smile. "And I have not at all rushed you to impart the information you have. Although I do believe this earth tremor has highlighted that time is not quite on our side."

Clark cast a sidelong look at Archie and silently hoped his friend wouldn't say anything to jeopardize the deal he had spent so long crafting.

"So you find Tarzan, figure out he's your cousin, and then you're just gonna hand over the Greystoke estate to him?" said Clark, carefully keeping his tone neutral. "That's mighty generous."

William smiled and slowly shook his head as if he had heard that comment a hundred times already. "I know how eccentric that may sound, but even without the estate's fortune, my side of the family is wealthy enough. I won't miss it."

Clark caught the slight quizzical lift of Archie's eyebrow and smiled. Archie knew a gift horse when he saw one.

William Greystoke continued. "Of course, I wish to find the aircraft and lay my aunt and uncle's bodies to rest back in England. With John—I'm sorry, as you call him, Tarzan—"

"That's what he calls himself," Archie cut in.

"Such an amusing moniker, don't you think? His real name is

John Clayton. Named after his father. Or he was to be. . . . I confess that I still have my doubts such a person exists. It's almost too preposterous to imagine."

"Oh, he's real, all right," said Clark, leaning back in his chair. "More so than you or me, I sometimes think. He's your boy, no matter how unlikely that sounds. And we have a deal, do we not?"

William raised his hands in a conciliatory manner. "Forgive me, I do not wish to cast doubt on what you believe, but we have had a fair number of charlatans making similar claims in the past. Once I talk to . . . Tarzan, a simple DNA test will confirm his authenticity. It's a little more reliable than a fingerprint." He chuckled at some private joke.

"We've had our fair share of nut jobs too," said Archie tersely. Only a few weeks earlier a Russian hunter had connived his way into the camp, only to steal a gorilla and send Tarzan, Robbie, and Jane on a hair-raising journey, the details of which he didn't want to find out. There were some things that parents should never know if they wanted to sleep at night.

"Ah, Nikolas Rokoff," said William in a low voice. "A nasty piece of work. A very deluded man." He didn't need to continue. Since he had arrived at the camp he had taken great pains to distance himself from the hunter.

"And once Tarzan's identity has been confirmed . . . ?" probed Clark. "Y'know we didn't talk specifics, but I recall a lot of zeroes on those emails."

William Greystoke studied Clark. In the past, Clark had faced down criminals, bloodthirsty rebel soldiers, and charging elephants. But under Greystoke's gaze, Clark got a fleeting feeling that he was nothing more than prey. He shook that thought away. Greystoke had been nothing but patient and generous since he had arrived.

"I admire a man who cuts to the heart of business. I am a businessman myself," Greystoke said. "Yes, there is a substantial reward for the *proven* return of Lord Greystoke. One million pounds." His gaze flicked across to Archie who was coughing up a lungful of beer. The thought of the money spread a wide smile across Clark's face, revealing his yellowed teeth. Greystoke dropped his voice close to a whisper. "With that kind of money, you could leave all this behind. Start a new life wherever you wished." His voice rose back to normal as he smiled. "Of course, if you want me to wait another week here, then so be it."

Archie cut in before Clark could say anything. "No need to wait. I think we should be able to get things rolling tomorrow." He looked at his old friend. Clark gave a small nod. Neither man wanted Greystoke in their camp any longer than necessary.

William shook Archie's hand, then took Clark's crushing grip. Archie's smile didn't falter as he glanced across at his daughter in the corner. But Clark could read his friend's mind. Between them and a million pounds lay some harsh jungle, and a pair of brooding teenagers.

• • •

"Absolutely not!" snapped Jane.

Archie sighed. "Jane, you're being unreasonable. . . ."

"I'm being unreasonable? Every time you bring somebody back, I'm proved right! That guy is not to be trusted!"

Archie, Clark, Jane, and Robbie had slipped across to the office, the largest cabin in the camp, where pay was dealt out and logging operations planned. Two bare bulbs were the only lights; the close-by generator's noisy hum was ever-present. The walls were covered in maps that were plotted with the locations of rare and valuable trees. Jane sat on the edge of Archie's desk, her arms folded. Robbie sat just behind her on the chair, his head cradled in his hands. He was tired and had heard these arguments before. Archie paced the room, trying to keep his temper in check, while Clark sat in the corner, one hand absently massaging his scarred leg as he glared at Jane from under his bushy eyebrows.

"His family has a seat in the British House of Lords—he's almost royalty, and you think he can't be trusted?"

"She's right," said Robbie. "The Greystokes paid Rokoff to hunt down Tarzan. They accused D'Arnot of being a fraud when he first tried to spread the world about a surviving heir." Robbie had learned a lot about D'Arnot, the French UN peacekeeper who had been saved by Tarzan and, in turn, had educated him and taught him to speak. The two had been good friends, until the day D'Arnot had decided to head back to civilization. But the modern world was more ruthless than the jungle had been, and nobody believed the Frenchman's tales. On his return to the jungle, he was murdered by Nikolas Rokoff, never to see his ape-man friend again. "What makes you think things have changed now?"

"The man just saved my life!" snapped Archie. "And you're talking about William's father, not him. He's only recently taken the title. He's already told us about Rokoff. The Russian was nothing more than a con artist, using the Greystokes as much as he used us."

Jane threw her hands in the air melodramatically. "And you believe him? Sometimes I wonder how we can be related!"

A hurt expression crossed Archie's face, but it was Clark who spoke up, unable to keep the spite from his voice.

"Y'know somethin', sweetheart? I wonder that sometimes too. I can only figure out that you took your mum's brains—and she was dumb enough to run away."

Being reminded of how Jane's mother had abandoned them stung. She had left without a word, leaving them with debt so severe that Archie had been forced to abandon his life as a doctor and turn to more lucrative, if illegal, activities so they could start all over again.

"It's no surprise you want in on this. Wasn't it your idea, anyway?" Jane snapped. "How much is he offering to pay you?"

"A million quid," said Clark levelly. "Just to hand back Tarzan's title. And if he don't wanna live in England, then he's free to stay 'ere. The only difference will be that we're not 'ere; we're someplace else and rich." Clark leaned forward in his chair. "And let's make one thing clear, missy." He poked a finger at her. "I've had about enough of you constantly sabotagin' not just your dad's happiness, but mine too. We've been good enough to ask your opinion, but we don't need it. Y'see, I know where the plane went down." He gestured to the jungle in general and grinned when Jane glanced at Robbie who leaned guiltily back in his chair.

"Even before Robbie got to see it for 'imself, I had the GPS coordinates of where Rokoff tagged Tarzan. That's how the Russian knew where to find Karnath. That's how I know where we're gonna lead his lordship."

Nobody except Clark could face Jane's accusing stare. With a sharp intake of breath she darted from the cabin.

"Jane, wait!" shouted Archie.

"Leave her be," said Clark. "She's not stupid enough to waltz into the jungle at night. Besides, where will she go, eh?" Clark stood, wincing as his injured leg took his weight. "We should all have an early night. Tomorrow's the day we all turn very rich."

• • •

The next morning, Robbie searched the camp for Jane, but was not surprised to see her gone. In the past he would have worried, but he knew exactly where she was headed. Jane must have made a break for it in the pre-dawn light, a time when the soft hues bathed the misty jungle, giving it a magical edge. He hooked a machete to his belt and followed Jane's faint spoor through the foliage. She had learned to move through the jungle without leaving too many signs of passing, and Robbie was beginning to worry he had made a mistake until, after an hour, the trail opened up into the Dum-Dum.

It was a wide clearing that was nothing more than a dust bowl, bordered on one side by a smooth curving cliff some thirty feet high. Several hollow logs lay in the dust, their trunks long devoured by insects, forming natural drums, which Tarzan had shown Jane how to beat to call him in times of danger. The pounding rhythm was amplified by the concave cliff and carried across the jungle for many miles.

Jane sat glumly on one log, staring at the surrounding trees. She didn't turn around when Robbie entered the clearing. He realized she'd heard his almost-silent approach and swore she had picked up on some of the incredible heightened skills Tarzan possessed.

"He's not coming," she said in almost a whisper.

"Call again."

She shook her head and turned to him. She was worried. Her long blonde hair had hastily been tied into a ponytail, and her face was still smudged with dirt from the previous day.

"They will find the plane, but they won't find him there," she said.

Robbie felt his cheek flush with guilt. It was his fault they knew where to look. "Jane, I'm sorry. . . ."

"No need. I know you thought differently then. . . . Thought you were doing the right thing."

Robbie nodded. When he had first met Tarzan, he hadn't warmed to the ape-man. It wasn't until he had joined Jane and Tarzan in their search for the kidnapped ape, Karnath, that he got to know the wild man. The many perils they faced had formed a bond as strong as a familial one. Robbie didn't want to see any harm befall his friend any more than Jane did. He still felt slivers of guilt every time he thought back to how he had planned to betray Tarzan.

"How do you know he's not there?" asked Robbie.

"He took me to a place he intended to take his family for food."

Robbie recalled Jane had mentioned something about a volcano; Clark had heard her say that too, but now didn't feel like the time to bring it up.

"So what do we do?"

Jane looked thoughtful, then smiled. "Perhaps we should let them find the airplane. Maybe that will be enough. . . ."

"You think we should go with them?" said Robbie in surprise.

A smile broke Jane's worried frown and she suddenly looked full of life again. "Better than that. We're going to really *help* them."

3

The rush of the wind was the only thing the ape-man could hear as he ran along a slender bough no wider than his foot. The hundred-foot drop below meant nothing to him. He didn't stop his breakneck pace even as the branch drooped under his weight. He had run through the trees all his life and could read the steady pulse of the wood through the soles of his feet. As the branch bent even lower, Tarzan tensed his powerful thigh muscles and leaped.

The branch acted like a springboard, catapulting him high into the air and out across the canopy of trees. His eyes were locked on to his landing area ahead—he knew with solid certainty where he would fall.

His feet crashed through the leafy canopy, startling a small knot of *manu*. The monkeys screeched at him as they fled from his path. Tarzan only had to use one hand to reach for a branch to stabilize himself as he hopped from branch to branch and carouseled around the huge trunk of a tree. Almost as fast as a man sprinting on the ground below, he jumped into the branches of an interlocking tree where he brachiated almost as fast as he could run—before dropping several feet onto a limb.

Ahead, through the dense leaves, he caught sight of a shock of coarse gray hair as the Targarni he was pursuing knuckled on all fours through the undergrowth, oblivious to his presence. Once again the Targarni had struck the Mangani, and their constant frays were beginning to test Tarzan's patience, like a tick that couldn't be scratched. He knew the Targarni numbered enough to evict the Mangani from the territory if they wished, so Tarzan was puzzled as to why they insisted on only small skirmishes.

After almost an hour, he sensed he was close to the heart of the Targarni's home. He could smell their stale stench, even through the odor of the foul Thunder Mountain. Tarzan paused at the top of a crooked tree that bent out from the slope of the mountain below, offering an unrivaled view of the land.

The volcano's peak rose behind him, and he judged himself to be close to the edge of the trees, near the barren scree slopes that took the brunt of the red rocks occasionally ejected from the cone. Thin plumes of gray smoke rolled from the cone, but Tarzan was accustomed to the sight. Here the soil was rich, and the jungle more lush than the valley below.

Tarzan remained stock-still, absorbing the world around him. The sounds of the jungle were comforting. Nothing was amiss, yet the smell of the Targarni assured him danger was at hand. A pair of *neeta* dropped onto the branch close to him and ruffled their bright yellow feathers as they preened. They didn't consider Tarzan a threat, just part of the scenery, so didn't notice him slink to the ground.

Using a trailing liana, Tarzan gently lowered himself without a sound. Doubled over, he stealthily ran up the slope, toward the strengthening scent of Targarni. Every one of his senses was now pulsing—something was very wrong. He crouched behind a boulder and peered over the top.

The ground beyond was shrouded in a fine mist. The trees thinned out, clinging to a network of large rocks that sprouted among the jungle. It took a moment for the stone's regularity to register with Tarzan, and he suddenly realized what he was looking at was the work of man, not nature. Even the boulder he was hunkering behind was several huge square stone blocks carefully fitted together. There was no obvious pattern to the ruins. They were nothing like the geometric shapes he had seen in the city or even in Jane's camp. There were images carved into the rock, most so weatherworn it was impossible to discern what they were supposed to be.

Tarzan had no interest in pictures. Emerging from behind the boulder, he took several cautious steps forward. Through the mist, he could see that there was something ahead, but could not quite make out what it was. The volcanic fumes and mist were rendering Tarzan's honed senses almost useless. Then he froze.

A pair of massive claws protruded from the undergrowth, perhaps a lion's, but it was difficult to tell. Nevertheless, they represented a beast the size of the trees. His heart pounded, but he held his ground long enough to see that the claws were made from stone. Between them lay a black void, an entrance of some kind. It was from there that the unpleasant smell emanated. Tarzan recognized it as the stench of death.

Tarzan quickly retreated. His thoughts on the Targarni were blacker than ever and uncertainty gnawed at him. Had he made a mistake bringing his family there?

• • •

Lord William Greystoke had taken Jane's offer to accompany them with a charming smile and assurances that he only meant to help his cousin and not hinder him. Clark took her sudden change in attitude with a huge amount of scepticism. His brow furrowed further when Jane apologized to him for losing her temper.

It took several hours for the expedition to pack their gear. William Greystoke played his part helping others, not once complaining. It was a move that gained the respect of Archie and the loggers, who expected the lord to consider himself above such things.

By 10 a.m., Greystoke, Archie, Robbie, and Jane were ready,

delayed only by Clark, who had difficulty shouldering his heavy supplies due to his injured leg. Even though they expected to be away for no more than two days, the supplies would last them for a week should anything unexpected happen. Archie tried to convince Clark to stay behind.

"An' miss out on the fortune an' glory?" hissed Clark as pain shot through his leg. "Not a chance, mate. Not a chance." He swallowed painkillers and wordlessly hefted his backpack over his shoulders, now made lighter by losing two days' worth of backup supplies. "We could all do with losin' a few pounds anyway," he commented, patting his stomach when Robbie questioned the rash action.

Mr. David had wanted to come, but Archie needed him to run the camp while they were away. Jane would have felt safer if he had come. She didn't trust Greystoke at all. She had read up on the family and was all too aware of their merciless streak. There was nothing she liked about the English lord and could all too easily imagine his cruel intentions.

The sun shone through the canopy, casting a network of shadows across their trail and providing welcome shade from the harsh sunlight. Despite misgivings, Jane and Robbie felt good to be traveling again and led from several yards ahead. They followed a trail that bypassed the Dum-Dum and snaked up a gentle hillside. After three hours, their clothes were damp with sweat and, with Clark lagging behind, Archie called for a break. On a plateau, they could see the jungle spread out beneath them, broken by a patchwork of brown rivers that vanished into the distance, joining the mighty Congo River somewhere over the horizon.

Robbie couldn't keep the smile off his face as he confided in Jane. "If you would've asked me a couple of months ago if I enjoyed hacking through all this . . ." he shook his head. "Now I just don't want to go back. Know what I mean?"

Jane didn't have the words to reply. She just smiled and took in the vista; she knew exactly what he meant. Out here was freedom, away from rules and regulations, far from the nightmares that had haunted them both back in so-called civilization. Their near-death experiences had lit a fire within them that made them feel more alive than ever before.

Archie and Clark broke out the cooking gear and soon had food bubbling away. Greystoke walked in a slow circle, holding a GPS device above his head as he searched for a signal. "Blasted thing!" he muttered.

Robbie smirked. The previous night he had broken into Greystoke's equipment and carefully unscrewed the device, breaking a single wire that connected to the antenna—rendering the GPS useless.

"Are you sure we're headed the right way?" Greystoke said, casting a suspicious sidelong glance at Jane.

"Pretty much."

"*Pretty much?*" His voice was cold. "Out here there is no margin for error, my dear."

Jane's smile dropped and she glared at him. "There are also no street signs, your lordship."

She saw her father raise a hand to cover the smile on his face, but Clark's eyes narrowed and he reached for the GPS.

"Gimme that. She knows. They both do. Two heads better than one, eh?" He examined the GPS, carefully rolling it in his hand and giving both Jane and Robbie a suspicious look.

Archie spoke up. "Well, we need to get going. I don't like the look of those clouds." He indicated the black swirl that had appeared over the mountain peak behind them. The weather was unpredictable at the best of times, but the glowering cumulonimbus above looked ominous.

• • •

The rain came in leaden sheets so heavy that the group could only see a few yards in front of them. Their path meandered close to a sharp slope that dropped to a cliff below, so the reduced visibility was more than an inconvenience.

Ponchos had been broken out, snugly fitting over their backpacks but doing little to keep anyone's legs dry below the knees. The ground rapidly changed from parched leaves to mud that sucked them down to their ankles and slowed progress. Rivulets of water trickling down the mountainside soon sprang into fast-flowing streams with enough force to sweep their feet from under them.

"Are you sure this is the way?" shouted Clark from over pattering rain that sounded as if the forest canopy was ready to collapse on them. His injured leg was forcing him to the back of the group with Robbie.

Robbie squinted, the rain stinging his eyes. "Think so. We really need the sun to check the direction." The driving rain drowned out any response from Clark, but as Robbie wiped his eyes he was startled to see the large man was bearing quickly down on him despite his injured leg. He wiped his eyes clear just as Clark roughly grabbed his shoulder and pulled him so close he could smell the man's stale breath.

"Listen 'ere, mate," Clark hissed as low as he could. "This ain't no game. This is serious cash that's gonna get us all out of this hellhole and we don't need you screwin' it up!"

Robbie shook him off. He was too surprised by Clark's sudden violent streak; this from the man who had found him stowed away on a cargo ship and offered him unquestioned help and friendship. Was the lure of being so close to the riches he'd always wanted now distorting Clark's priorities? Robbie's mind wondered, trying to make sense of it all, before he realized Archie was shouting a warning.

"Guys!"

Robbie glanced up just in time and saw the earth move through the trees uphill. Archie and Greystoke were already scrambling for cover from what was approaching. Rain stung Robbie's eyes again, forcing them shut—but not before he heard the low rumble of the mudslide as it rushed toward them like a freight train. The previous earth tremors had dislodged a huge chunk of earth higher up and the sudden rain had been all that was needed to turn it to liquid.

Robbie turned to run, blindly grabbing for Clark who was frozen to the spot, staring up at the wall of mud and debris piling toward them.

"Clark!" Robbie could say no more before he felt the ground pulled from beneath his feet as the mudslide poured into him. He felt himself falling backward, and caught a brief glimpse of Jane reaching for him with one hand, the other securing her to a sturdy tree limb, before he tumbled onto his back.

Robbie reached out for anything to which he could anchor himself, but his hands cut through the shifting mud. He could feel it everywhere—in his eyes, his ears, even seeping into his mouth.

He lost all sense of direction as he spun around. Something soft bounced into him and ricocheted away—Clark? He tried to reach for it, but his grasp was slick. Then he struck something hard—a tree. His breath was knocked out of him as he spun around the object. Before he could get a grip, the muddy torrent bore him away again, glancing his shoulder off another tree before his stomach lurched and he dropped like a stone. With a sickening sense of dread, he knew he had been dragged over the cliff.

· · ·

To Jane, it felt as if her arm was being yanked from her socket as she held on to the tree, the mudslide flowing beneath her, pulling at her legs. For almost half a minute there seemed to be no end to the torrent—until it suddenly petered out to a trickle then stopped. The trail they had been on was now five feet higher, a slick wedge of mud that led from the mountain above to the drop below.

Even though the avalanche had stopped, Jane didn't dare let go of the branch. She fought for breath, still shocked at seeing Robbie and Clark dragged away in an instant.

"Jane!"

Archie emerged from a knot of trees, Greystoke following closely behind. The backs of both men were covered in glossy mud from where they had hidden from the deluge.

"Dad!" Seeing Archie finally gave Jane the strength to release the branch. She caught her balance in the mud and ran across to hug him. With every step she took, the mud shifted beneath her boots and her arms windmilled, keeping her balanced.

"Where are the others?" asked Greystoke with concern, although Jane had no doubt he was only worried about being left out here alone.

"They were swept over," she answered as the reality hit her: They could be dead. That was how the jungle usually claimed its victims, with swift attacks. Normally she had no time to let the danger sink in before it had passed, but now she felt sick at the thought of losing her friends.

"ROBBIE!" she yelled, trying to move closer to the edge of the slope to see over.

Two steps were all it took for the mud beneath her to ebb forward, slowly pulling her toward the brink. She tried to remove a foot to backtrack, but the mud held it fast and she inched toward the inevitable drop.

"Hold on!" yelled Greystoke.

She turned to see him yanking his poncho off, and dropping his backpack to the floor. He was already soaked to the skin as he freed the climbing rope bundled to the bottom of the pack.

Once again, Jane struggled in the mud, but it held her tight. She turned back to see Greystoke swing the rope with one hand.

"Grab hold!" he shouted as he let go of one end.

Jane caught it, instantly twisting it around her wrist for extra security, and slid to a halt. Archie held the rope as Greystoke backed toward the trees to get a firmer footing.

"I'll pull you back."

Jane shook her head. "No. I've got to see what happened to the others."

"Jane," said Archie, his voice breaking with concern. "We can do that. First I want you to come back where it's safer."

"So you can go over the edge to look?" Despite the fear she felt she couldn't help but give a short laugh. "And who's going to hold the rope? Me?"

Archie knew his parental responsibility was to argue, but she was right. Before he could even answer, Jane had tied the rope around her waist and held the trailing cord with one hand.

"OK, give me some slack."

Archie glanced at Greystoke who shrugged—it wasn't his decision. Archie muttered under his breath, then composed himself. "OK, go easy though."

Jane edged toward the slope, leaning as far forward as she could. She called for more slack and reached the incline. It was a good seventy degrees, possibly more. The mud had carried debris through the trees, some of which had wedged in low-hanging branches. Rain flowed over the waterlogged mud in fast-flowing streams. Descent without the rope would be impossible, even with it . . .

Then she saw a shock of color poking through the mud about thirty feet below. It was the unmistakable red of Clark's poncho, but he wasn't moving.

"Clark?" Jane's voice sounded small, drowned out by the heavy rain. She tried again, louder: "CLARK!"

For a moment he didn't stir. Then he looked up. Only the whites of his eyes were clearly visible beneath his mud mask. It was so comical, Jane nearly laughed aloud. "Are you hurt?"

"Of course I'm bloody hurt!" he snapped back with enough grumpiness to tell Jane he was fine.

"Where's Robbie?" her voice almost broke as she said his name. Robbie had changed so much since she first met him that she now couldn't imagine not having him around.

"He's down 'ere," said Clark gruffly. "But he ain't comin' up."

Jane didn't like the sound of that. "I'm coming down!"

Archie put up a feeble show of trying to stop her, but there was no other choice. He tied one end of his own rope to a tree and tossed it to Jane so she could attach it to Clark. Jane turned around, holding her rope with both hands as she carefully stepped backward. With each step she risked falling flat on her face, so she didn't rush her descent. Twice she had to clamber over stumps wedged between trees before she reached Clark.

He had been caught by a huge low-sweeping bough that had hooked him up from danger. She helped him wipe the mud off his face and saw he was cut and bruised, but in one piece. His backpack had taken the brunt of the impact as he had pinballed down the slope. She tied the second rope under his arms and waited as her own line was tied to a tree so both Greystoke and Archie could haul Clark back up the incline.

It took a good ten minutes before Clark was safe and the men could once again lower Jane down. The rain began to ease a little, although all that did was offer a better view of the sheer drop she was approaching. Being with Tarzan had given her a head for heights, but for some reason, even though she had a rope tied to her, standing on the muddy slope felt much less safe than soaring through the treetops a hundred feet above.

The incline suddenly gave way to a sheer cliff where mud slopped over the edge in a slow waterfall. Jane collected herself, gathering her confidence before leaning back over the edge and peering down.

The cliff dropped for several hundred feet, vanishing into the canopy below. Ten feet down, Robbie lay on his back—by some miracle caught from plummeting to his death on a lone curving trunk that clung to a gap in the rock face. It was barely big enough for him, and sagged under his weight. He didn't dare move; instead he stared straight ahead, not risking a look at Jane.

"Took your time," he said with forced jollity.

Jane grinned, her confidence growing. "You just sit back and let me do all the work. As usual." She called up for more slack, which she looped under her arms as she had done when learning to rappel one summer camp, long ago.

"Not a bad view," she said casually as she rappelled the first few feet.

Robbie didn't have time to answer because the trunk he was lying on suddenly cracked and he dropped. . . .

4

Jane didn't pause to assess the situation. She acted on pure instinct, as she had been forced to do ever since she'd got lost in the jungle. Mustering the strongest kick she could, she leaped from the cliff.

Her eyes didn't leave Robbie as she flew toward him, the rope whipping out behind her. The rush of air was deafening and rain stung her face, as painful as the pelt of small stones.

Time seemed to slow as the breaking branch under Robbie sagged. The wood didn't fully break, but he'd reached the tipping point and flipped backward off the branch with a scream.

In less than two seconds, Jane cannoned into him in mid-air—so hard that the breath was knocked from him and his scream turned into a wheeze. She wrapped both her arms and legs tightly around him as the slack in the rope suddenly snapped tight, constricting around her waist with such ferocity Jane yelped, convinced she would be sliced in half. Instead, their rapid descent stopped. Robbie's additional weight pulled at her limbs and she could already feel him slipping from her arms as they swung like a pendulum back toward the cliff—

They slammed hard into the rock face, the brunt of the impact taken by Robbie's backpack. Caught like a fish on a line, they rotated lazily around before the rope began slowly lowering. Jane tried to recall if her father had tied it to a tree. Or was their combined weight now pulling him, Greystoke, and Clark through the mud?

Robbie found his croaky voice. "Now what?"

Jane could still feel him slowly slipping through her arms. She clenched her legs tighter. She was probably crushing the air from him, but he wasn't complaining.

"Your pack—it's too heavy!" she said through gritted teeth.

Even as she spoke, Robbie had spotted the problem. He tried to move his arms to shuck it off, but Jane held him in a vice-like bear hug.

"You're gonna have to let go of me," he said urgently.

Jane hesitated, unsure if her legs alone would be enough to support him. The rope suddenly jolted, lowering them a couple more feet. They had no choice. She nodded—then unlocked her arms.

No longer supported, Robbie's torso dropped straight down, pulled by the weight of his pack. He scrambled to remove his poncho. It caught across his face, but he managed to throw it off, the bright yellow material fluttering away on the wind. He pulled his arms from the straps, but the pack still refused to fall. Cursing loudly, he remembered fastening the pack's strap around his waist to stop it rubbing as he walked. His fingers were numb as he worked at the plastic catch.

"Hurry!" shouted Jane as they inched farther downward. As both their legs were covered in mud, she could feel Robbie slowly slipping away. She could only imagine the chaos up on the slope as the three men struggled to restrain the rope with slippery, muddy hands.

Robbie tried again, arcing his body so he could see the clip even if he couldn't feel it. He pressed the plastic release again and his backpack suddenly fell far away. Straining his abs, Robbie lunged closer to Jane and they threw their arms around each other in a fierce bear hug—they had never been so close—just as his slick legs slipped through hers and he dangled precariously over the void.

"Things haven't improved," he said through gritted teeth.

That wasn't entirely correct—at least they had stopped inching lower. An eternity seemed to pass when there was a sudden yank on the rope and they rapidly ascended in a series of jerky movements.

Before long they were hauled back up to the incline where they could see Archie, Clark, and Greystoke heaving at the rope, which they had looped around a tree to form a pulley.

Nobody spoke as they were hauled to safety. All five figures sat back and caught their breath, thankful to be alive. Jane realized it was the first time she could remember being in peril in the jungle that Tarzan hadn't shown. She only hoped that meant he was far away from the aircraft, safely out of Lord William Greystoke's clutches.

. . .

The campfire dried out their damp clothes and attracted insects; it was the only beacon in the inky darkness. Robbie watched as a flying bug the size of his fist crawled across the floor between him and Jane. It was so close to her that she should have freaked out—would have freaked out in the past—but now she simply watched it clean its slender antennae. After saving his life, he had only managed a simple "thanks." Anything more seemed inappropriate.

Lord Greystoke wildly swatted around his head as flies and beetles hummed past him. He was a man used to the luxuries of life. Archie cooked supper over the fire and Clark nursed his injuries as he tinkered with Greystoke's GPS.

"Is it always like this?" said Greystoke, his voice already wary as he indicated the darkness around him.

"No, it's normally far worse," Robbie replied when nobody else spoke up.

A piercing caw suddenly rose from the trees, causing Greystoke to flinch. "What the hell is that?"

The others didn't react; it was an all-too-familiar sound. "Monkey," said Robbie absently. "I thought you'd been out here before? With your 'business interests'?"

Greystoke flailed at the bugs circling him. "Not so rugged a venture, I'm afraid. Helicopters and air-conditioned jeeps are the way one travels with any degree of civilization."

Jane didn't flinch as the slender insect moved closer to her foot and slowly crawled up her leg. "Why bother coming out here to find him?" she asked suddenly. "Why not leave him in peace?"

Greystoke couldn't take his eyes off the creature on Jane's leg. All he could see was a slobbering, disease-carrying beast.

"Because he's family," said Greystoke eventually. "He needs to be given the choice."

Jane smirked, and Greystoke focused his intense gaze on her. Gone was the mask of a confounded Englishman, replaced by a ruthless, calculating businessman. "If it was one of your family out here: your father, your mother, perhaps . . ."

Jane flinched at the mention of her mother. Robbie suspected it was a deliberate cheap shot designed to provoke a reaction.

"Wouldn't you want to know they were safe?" Greystoke continued. "To afford them every opportunity of joining the real world rather than living out here as a savage?"

The locust on Jane's leg suddenly took flight, circling toward Greystoke.

"He won't come. He won't speak to you," muttered Jane. Her voice was barely audible over the crackling campfire, but Greystoke had heard her. Without looking away from her, he swatted the locust. The delicate insect was batted into the fire, its body popping as it ignited.

"He will," said Greystoke in icy tones. "Something you will come to understand, my dear, is that I always get my way."

The GPS in Clark's hand bleeped to life. He had removed the back of the device, using his penknife to unscrew it, and had reconnected the sabotaged wire. Numbers flashed on the display screen.

"Bingo! You had some faulty wirin' in there; no wonder this thing wasn't workin," he said, handing the device to Greystoke, but glaring accusingly at Robbie.

Greystoke studied the coordinates and his shoulders sagged. "This can't be right."

"What's wrong?" said Archie looking up from the simmering food that was now making Robbie's stomach rumble.

"According to the GPS we're farther away from the site than when we began!" He glared at Jane and Robbie. Robbie looked away, knowing he'd betray them, but Jane held his gaze.

"How do you know where we're headed?" she said flatly. "I thought you needed Clark for that?"

Greystoke's expression didn't falter as Archie and Clark gazed questioningly at him.

"I obtained the information," he said curtly.

"From where?" probed Robbie.

It was as if the jungle had hushed in order to hear Greystoke. The fire popped and crackled before he spoke up. "I bought it from a hunter who came across the aircraft."

"Rokoff," said Jane with certainty. The mention of the Russian hunter caused Greystoke to flinch as if he'd been struck. Jane pressed on, enjoying Greystoke's discomfort. "You hired him, didn't you? You paid him to come up here—" her voice grew louder with each word as her temper flared.

"Jane!" snapped Archie. "Enough."

Greystoke spoke before she could continue. "My father employed his services on a number of occasions, but I had nothing to do with the unfortunate Ugandan affair. If anything that just gave these gentlemen's claims about Tarzan's possible heritage"—he indicated Robbie and Clark—"more credence."

Jane flicked a look at Robbie. Even after all the danger they had been through together, Robbie had been surprised that she had so readily forgiven him for trying to prove Tarzan's existence to the Greystokes. He had finally decided it was the wrong thing to do, by which time Clark had already invited the English lord to their camp. Robbie and Jane both knew Rokoff had confessed to killing Tarzan's friend and mentor, D'Arnot, under the orders of Greystoke's father.

"We lost what? Maybe half a day?" said Archie levelly. "I figure the little incident on the pass must've scrambled everybody a little. Now's not the time to throw accusations around."

"Suppose not," muttered Jane who, for once, didn't challenge her father.

Robbie saw her look up to the surrounding trees when she thought nobody was looking. He knew what she sensed: the same thing as him. They were being watched.

As Archie shared out the basic rations, Robbie tried to ignore the pain from the bruises across his body. He was knew that was Tarzan watching over them. He would sleep soundly tonight.

• • •

Tarzan watched the pale light flickering in the darkness and felt a tremor of nerves, something he had not felt since his early years. Back then, he could take refuge by his mother's side. Kala was the ape that had found him in the jungle and raised him as her own. She had long since died, and now Tarzan was responsible for the entire band of apes—and the glow in the darkness troubled him.

Through many seasons the mountain had spewed glowing rock, or lava—he recalled the name Jane had given for it when he'd last brought her there. But the frequency had increased since the Mangani's arrival and Tarzan wondered if it was some Targarni trick. Did they have a special power over the fire rock?

The Targarni had not made an appearance since Tarzan had tracked them back to their lair. He had expected another violent confrontation—brute force was the way of the jungle when scores needed to be settled—but the apes had remained quiet.

Tarzan tried to calm himself. He desperately needed sleep, and all around him he could hear the rustling of the apes and the occasional wheeze as they slept in their nests. The females and younglings were woven among branches in the trees, while a few of the young silverbacks and the heavy Kerchak remained on the ground. They were safe enough, even if the Targarni chose to spring an attack.

Tarzan curled up in a mossy nook in the base of a tree's great roots. He felt sleep take its hold. In that fleeting moment he wondered where Jane was. She was out there, somewhere in the darkness. . . .

• • •

"A ll our provisions have gone!" growled Clark, throwing his backpack down. "All of 'em!"

They'd awoken to a cool misty morning to discover that their backpacks had been looted and the expedition provisions had been taken. Everything was gone; from the general supplies Clark and Archie had been carrying, down to the energy bars they all had in their separate packs.

"Is this him? Tarzan?" said Greystoke with a gleam in his eye as he studied the trees. They looked uninviting as the mist crept between the mighty boles.

" 'Course it is," snarled Clark. "He used to sabotage our camp to try 'n' scare us away. Even set fire to it once. Man's an animal."

Jane was confused. Tarzan was a trickster and could be mischievous, but this made no sense. Why take the food? If anything it would harm the people he cared for—and would do nothing to slow Greystoke's quest.

Greystoke retrieved the GPS from his tent. "We still have this . . . and a signal. A little weak due to the weather, but at least it works."

"We can't push on without supplies," said Archie. "If we're lucky we can make it back to camp before nightfall. . . ."

Clark waved his hand vigorously to cut off that line of thought. "No way. That's what he wants us to do. We push on. Another half day or so and we get to the plane."

Archie paused. Clark seldom disagreed so forcefully. "That puts us farther from the food," he pointed out.

"Well, I guess that's settled then," said Robbie as he began to pack his gear away. "Let's head home."

"You're jokin', right?" said Clark. "I know you've lived off the land before." He stabbed a finger at Jane. "And you certainly know how to find a three-course meal out here." He drew a hunting knife from a sheath strapped to his shin. "An' I've hunted a fair bit o' game in my time. His lordship 'ere might be a bit out of his depth, but we ain't turnin' back. Right, Arch?" He stared at Archie, an unspoken communication between two old friends, fueled by the huge reward that was just within their grasp. For a moment it looked as if Archie were about to disagree, but he finally nodded.

"Sure," said Archie. "We know what we're doing." The last comment was aimed at Greystoke, an assurance that their services were worth the obscene amount of reward money.

With practiced ease, they packed the rest of the camp away in a matter of minutes—although Archie had to help Greystoke fold his tent like some giant piece of origami. The man's privileged upbringing meant he had never had to do very much for himself. They trudged toward the mist-veiled trees, led by Clark who held the GPS. He walked more slowly than ever since the mudslide incident, his limp more pronounced. Jane and Robbie trailed behind.

"Nice try," Robbie whispered.

Jane looked at him with wide blue eyes. "It wasn't me."

"Yeah, right," sniggered Robbie. "At least tell me where you stashed the energy bars. I'm starving."

Jane grabbed his arm and pulled him to a stop. Her brow was furrowed with concern. "I didn't do this." She followed his gaze to the trees and added, in an ominous hushed tone, "And I don't think it was Tarzan either."

· · ·

The rest of the day progressed in relative silence. The mist increased the higher they climbed, swallowing every sound and covering everything with fine moisture that dampened and chilled to the bone. Even the jungle appeared to fall silent. Robbie couldn't recall hearing a bird chirp all day.

Jane's comments had made him jumpy. If Tarzan wasn't out there, who was? Who else had the skills to move like a ghost through the camp without waking any of them? He started seeing shadows in his peripheral vision, but every time he snapped his head around, they faded away. He'd wound himself up so much that at one point, when Jane leaned against his shoulder to steady herself on a particularly sharp incline, he yelped in surprise.

Clark's limp grew worse and he started involuntarily huffing from the pain with each step. He doggedly followed the GPS coordinates, guiding them through trails wherever he could. When they stopped to rest, all their stomachs warbled in chorus. Jane managed to find some edible fruits and nuts, but not enough to feed the five of them. It was clear that there would be no small game to hunt in the mist.

The slope became tougher, their progress slower—but then the GPS started to make a series of regular bleeping tones.

"We're close," breathed Clark, barely containing his excitement. "This way."

He guided them up a sharp incline that turned into a hairpin bend as it rose. The swirling mist rolled to one side, hinting at a great drop close by. Jane began to see familiar rock formations, but couldn't be sure until the GPS's tone became almost constant. Clark drew his pistol from his belt holster.

"You won't need that," hissed Jane.

"I just wanna make sure no hairy ape thinks he can charge me," said Clark in a low voice. Under Tarzan's guidance, the apes had helped free Clark and the other loggers from the clutches of a rebel leader, Tafari. They had been peaceful and benign to the loggers back them, but Clark hadn't been planning to take their leader away.

The ground flattened out, but all they could see was a bare plateau. Greystoke looked disappointed and took the GPS from Clark to check for himself. But Jane knew they were in the right place. Even before Greystoke could open his mouth to complain, the mist thinned ever so slightly—revealing the dark silhouette of a plane wreckage on the edge of the plateau. The damp mist gave a haunted feel to the place, and for the first time Jane wondered what had happened to the bodies of Tarzan's parents after the crash. Had they survived? Were they buried somewhere around the wreckage?

Clark and Archie high-fived each other as Greystoke took several faltering steps forward.

"My word . . ." said Greystoke with awed tones. "It's my uncle's plane. . . ."

The words had an odd effect on Jane. She had felt nothing but loathing toward the pompous man, but now she realized the dead occupants of the plane were his family, just as much as Tarzan really was. She began to doubt that interfering with Greystoke's goals was the right thing to do. A quick glance at Robbie told her he was thinking the same thing. For him, family had a far more emotional sting. After all, he was in the jungle to escape from the legacy of the nightmarish death of his sister, Sophie.

William Greystoke slowly advanced on the aircraft, keeping a wary eye out for any gorillas that might suddenly charge, but there were none. He ran a hand along the cracked and rusting fuselage. One wing had been torn off against the mountainside, hidden behind them, while the other projected over a cliff, although the end of it was veiled from view in the mist.

"He's gotta be around here someplace," said Clark, his pain forgotten as his enthusiasm surged. "And he's probably got our food round 'ere too." He cupped his hands around his mouth and shouted. "TARZAN!" The gray cloud swallowed the cry. He tried again: "TARZAN! IT'S CLARK. JANE'S 'ERE TOO!"

Nothing.

Jane shrugged and sat on a boulder, relieved to take her backpack off. "I told you he wouldn't want to speak to you. What're you going to do now, just sit here and wait?"

Greystoke ignored her. Instead, he paced around the aircraft with purpose. He stopped at the side, where a tear in the fuselage formed an artificial cave. The entrance was now covered in vines and foliage but there was just enough light for him to see some seats had been torn up and cast aside. The floor was covered in dry grass and tree branches, carefully laid down for the apes to sleep on. There was an overpowering smell that reminded him of a farmyard, and he scrunched his nose.

Reaching the aircraft's tail he saw the cargo door was torn open, allowing him access into the belly of the craft. Jane watched him intently as he disappeared inside. There she had found nothing but boxes with some scientific gear, rank clothing, and a few photographs of John Clayton, the Earl of Greystoke—Tarzan's father and William's uncle.

"HA!" exclaimed William Greystoke. Jane's suspicions ratcheted up as she heard a case being dragged through the hold. What had he found? He'd certainly made no attempt to call out to his long-lost cousin or shown any signs of searching for him.

Greystoke emerged from the hold, pulling a small plastic flight case. It was covered in filth from almost two decades of neglect. He laid it flat on the floor and fumbled the catches open.

Clark and Archie moved closer, puzzled by William's odd behavior.

"What've you got there?" said Archie as innocently as possible.

"What I've been searching for," intoned Greystoke as he applied more pressure on the catches. They finally snapped open.

"I thought you were looking for your cousin?" said Clark as delicately as he could.

Greystoke never looked up. "Mmm? Oh yes . . . yes. But this . . ." He lay his hand reverently on the surface of the case. "This is what *they* came for. My uncle and aunt . . ."

Robbie and Jane stood behind Lord William Greystoke as he slowly opened the case. Inside were two neat folders and, wedged between them, a wooden box. Being encased in plastic, nothing had aged at all. Greystoke gently brushed his fingers over the folders, then went for the wooden casket first. It was an oblong box, six inches long and as wide as his thumb. He slid the lid off, and a flurry of small gemstones cascaded to the floor. Even in the poor light they sparkled like a rainbow.

Clark whistled and dropped to his knees to inspect the haul. He held a yellow stone up for a closer look. "I ain't no gem expert, but I reckon they're worth a good few bucks."

"No doubt," said Greystoke dismissively. "But *this* is worth more."

He gently pulled a folder from the case and opened it up. Inside was a collection of handwritten notes. He rapidly flicked through with increasing excitement. Jane caught glimpses of diagrams, hand-drawn maps, and sketches of buildings.

"What is that?"

Greystoke quickly closed the book, suddenly aware that she'd seen the contents. He held it close to his chest.

"Details of the Savage Lands."

"Savage Lands?" repeated Robbie, confused.

Greystoke's voice dropped so low he was almost talking to himself. "They found it . . . they actually found it." The he remembered he had an audience. "My aunt and uncle were philanthropists, but they also loved stories, legends. . . . While they were out here they heard the legend of an ancient civilization and a lost city of unfathomable riches. Early explorers came looking for proof, but they died in the jungle, which is why this little patch of hell came to be called the Savage Lands. Few who step foot here return, as my uncle discovered. He and my aunt claimed to have found evidence of the civilization, but they were tight-lipped about the details. But this"— he held the folder tighter—"this is their research. In these pages lies the location of the heart of the lost empire: the city of Opar!"

5

Under Lord William Greystoke's guidance, Archie and Clark combed the plateau for any signs of Tarzan or the apes. Every indication they found—dry dung, gorilla nests, and a pile of half-chewed bones—indicated that the area hadn't been lived in for a week or so. Jane was relieved that Tarzan had moved his family on almost immediately after they last parted.

Greystoke didn't appear overly concerned that his cousin was not around. When pressed by Jane, he avoided answering. She noticed his evasiveness worried Clark, so took delight in mentioning it as often as she could. Eventually, with the thought of the reward money disappearing, Clark spoke up.

"So this was all about those survey documents? Not your cousin?"

"We should be going," said Greystoke, trying to step around Clark. Clark simply stepped to the side, blocking the man. Greystoke's eyes narrowed. Clark was an intimidating figure, but Greystoke was not used to being bullied.

"Not before we get some answers," said Clark in a low, gently threatening voice.

Greystoke wasn't intimidated. If anything, his expression turned to stone—but after a few moments a smile tugged his lips as he identified Clark's worry.

"Ah, your reward?"

"It had been playin' on my mind."

"For these documents alone you will get half of it, and Tarzan is still a concern—"

Archie smoothly cut in. "Well, for a city of unfathomable riches, that's a whole new deal. The finder's fee alone . . . surely worth more than a couple of million?"

Greystoke's smile faltered, his eyes flicking between Archie and Clark. "Of course, you will be compensated. As for Tarzan, personally, I don't care if my cousin is sitting out there thinking he's a monkey. However, business is business and if he does really exist—and after everything I have seen, I have no reason to doubt it—then certain contingents with my family think it prudent to find him. But we are hardly equipped to search any farther for him now, are we? He's made sure of that." Greystoke studied the trees, which gradually vanished into the mist. He was convinced Tarzan was out there, watching them. He could feel the eyes upon them.

"So let's head back to camp," said Robbie, absently massaging his shoulder.

"No," said Greystoke. Everybody looked at him in surprise. His tone was imperious as he pointed to Jane. "You led us on a merry romp in a circle, remember? And somebody tinkered with my GPS." He switched his cold gaze to Robbie. "And I am sure Tarzan is no electrical engineer. I have a facility beyond this range. A little farther than your camp, but the going is easier. Plus, as we draw nearer, I have arranged transport solutions." He selected another option on the GPS and a fresh set of coordinates appeared on the screen. As he passed Jane, he smirked, his voice dropping to a whisper. "Don't take me for a fool, my dear." To the others he waved his arm as he marched away. "Onward!"

Clark and Archie swapped a glance. Greystoke was obviously

playing them, and Clark hated being manipulated. But now the stakes had been raised, and with more money on the table, it was prudent to play along. Nobody spoke as they retrieved their packs and followed Greystoke back into the jungle.

. . .

The scent was unmistakable, even masked by the noxious fumes of Thunder Mountain. People. Tarzan had spent the morning patrolling the perimeter of the mountain flank the Mangani claimed as home, even venturing to the narrow gorge on the far side of the mountain where a dozen waterfalls cascaded from the walls, creating a myriad of rainbows. Today the mountain had calmed and the sense of danger from it had lessened, but now a new threat appeared.

Tarzan entered the trees midway down the mountain at a run. He kicked from one trunk to another, zigzagging higher until his hands could grasp the lower boughs. He was traveling so swiftly that his body looped around the first branch before he let go and somersaulted across the void to the next tree, landing on a branch in a crouch. Leaves rustled from the impact, and in a couple of seconds Tarzan was already ten yards above the ground and running through the branches.

The scent of people grew stronger, and with it, his caution increased. Never before had people come this far, except Jane, and he had needed to guide her there safely. He stopped in the boughs. Drooping leaves provided cover from prying eyes. The sound of approaching people grew, as loud as Tantor the jungle elephant, the clink of metal betraying their "civilized" origins, and they smelled worse than any wild animal. He could hear terse voices, but couldn't identify the language. It didn't take long for them to come into view. Like all hunters, Tarzan had deliberately chosen this location to stop because the clearing below offered a natural foraging area, or at least a place for people to rest.

There were four figures, one a female with light brown skin, cropped black hair, and a taller build than Jane. Their backpacks were almost as big as they were.

Tarzan felt for the rope looped around his waist, and then his hand slid to the dagger he kept sheathed there. It was his one advantage when facing the talons of jungle predators, and he had no qualms using it on humans. The people looked tired and irritated, and were arguing with one another. Three of them carried machetes to hack through the undergrowth, but one had a far worse weapon slung over his shoulder. It was short and boxy, the kind of thing from which Tarzan had seen Tafari's rebels shoot death. The man placed the weapon by his feet and wearily sat on a root, mopping perspiration from his brow.

So close to Tarzan's family, they were not welcome visitors. If he couldn't scare them away, then he would have no hesitation to using more deadly methods. He unsheathed his blade and calculated his best form of attack.

The group put their backpacks down, their argument increasing as they sat down to rest. The female sat at the base of Tarzan's tree and was arguing the loudest, before she shook her head and leaned back to rest. From her vantage point she could see straight up into the canopy of trees.

Tarzan froze—she was looking straight at him.

For a moment she didn't appear to see him through the hanging foliage, but then her brow furrowed as if she was trying to work out what it was she was looking at. Before she could open her mouth to speak, there was a sharp crack from deeper in the forest and everybody suddenly looked up, alert and tense. The man with the weapon snatched it from the floor and swung it onto his shoulder, aiming it toward the noise. They couldn't see what was out there, but Tarzan could: the Targarni. He had been so wrapped up in studying the humans that his enemies had managed to sneak in close.

Silence reigned. Then there was a burst of white fur and Goyad stormed from the undergrowth, bowling over the nearest man. The man flipped through the air and, with a snap of bones, landed hard on his back. Goyad's black jaws snapped shut across the man's throat, blood smattering the albino's snow-white fur and silencing the man's terrified screams.

Five more chimps bolted from the sides. Two grabbed another

man by his arms and legs and dragged him into the foliage, striking him unconscious.

Tarzan didn't flinch, didn't take his eyes off the attack. He had no emotional attachment to the people below. They were nothing more than two species of animal caught in the eternal jungle conflict, but he watched the unfolding battle with the eyes of a general. This was no mindless attack: Goyad was herding his warriors using his unusual intelligence.

Tarzan had expected the man with the weapon to open fire, but instead he stood frozen in terror—only having the presence of mind to swing the weapon across the head of the chimp attacking him. To Tarzan's surprise, the feeble weapon cracked into several pieces and the man was hurled to the ground.

Goyad gave several sharp hoots as the man finally backed toward the woman, both now pressed against a tree in terror. The albino ape stood taller than the other pale chimps. One eye was permanently swollen shut, the other a deep blood red.

The Targarni circled the two humans, fangs bared. Then they bolted forward and struck the humans across their heads.

Tarzan felt a twinge—of what? Regret? Sympathy?—as the female briefly looked up at him with pleading eyes before she was hit. However, the Targarni did not kill them; they had something more sinister in mind. For reasons Tarzan couldn't fathom, the apes dragged the three unconscious humans with them—taking them back to their lair as prisoners.

• • •

The atmosphere became more oppressive. The mist refused to clear, but lingered, becoming uncomfortably humid as Greystoke's party followed a trail around the mountain. After half a day's walk, the trail began to slowly descend. Robbie became vaguely aware that the rebel leader, Tafari, had had a camp just northwest of their position—but that was before Tarzan had summoned an army of animals and flattened it to the ground. He hoped the lands were safer now.

Although there was much to discuss, Clark and Archie were uncharacteristically quiet, doggedly following Greystoke. The lord himself occasionally checked the GPS to note their position, but said nothing.

Hours passed and the sky grew darker, and still the mist didn't lift. Hunger gnawed at them every time they sat to rest and if it wasn't for Jane's ability to gather edible fruits they would have starved. The only conversation came toward the end of the day when Archie finally told Greystoke they had to stop for the night. Robbie and Clark set up camp while Jane foraged for more food.

She didn't venture beyond the warm light of the campfire—the mist-veiled jungle was more ominous than she could ever recall. Tarzan had taught her to understand the jungle just by the sounds—the distinct audio landscape usually warned of danger. But right now it was sullenly quiet. Even the nighttime chorus of frogs and insects had failed to start. It was as if Tarzan's departure had sucked the life from the land. The forest felt abandoned, haunted even. Just as everybody settled at the campfire, Jane returned with an armful of fruit.

"I'd kill for somethin' hot," murmured Clark as he squeezed the fruit dejectedly.

"At my facility, I employ the finest chef, no expense spared. Not even out here," said Greystoke. He was the only one of the team who failed to pick up on the ominous calm around them.

"Is that right?" said Clark. "And what exactly do you do at this facility?"

"Make money," was the enigmatic reply.

Clark and Archie exchanged a glance, a humorless smile crossing Clark's face. "Good, because we have a deal, remember."

Under the flickering light, Greystoke examined the fruit Jane had handed him. "I may be many things, but I am not a businessman who goes back on his deals. I assure you, you will not be disappointed. We should be there by the afternoon."

Jane's eyes fell on the case Greystoke had retrieved from the aircraft. He'd kept it by his side the entire journey.

"So what were John and Alice Clayton doing out here?" Jane

asked, referring to Tarzan's parents. "I thought they were conservationists, not treasure hunters."

Greystoke snorted, a fleeting look of disdain crossing his face. "They fancied themselves as adventurers. Throwing the family fortune at hopeless causes. They spent hundreds of thousands trying to educate the Mbuti natives here. They're a bunch of simple imbeciles who could never be educated, so why bother?"

"You're a real saint," said Robbie sarcastically.

Greystoke's eyes narrowed. "Perhaps I should take lessons from you?" he said with venom. "It was Alice's fault. She married into the family and the next moment the fortune was being squandered. Such a bad influence. My father was distraught but there was nothing he could do. . . . Uncle John was close to flittering everything away. The family knew they had to take steps." He lapsed into silence, thoughtfully staring into the campfire.

Jane suddenly had an unsettling thought. "Take steps? You mean arrange for their plane to crash, maybe?"

Greystoke didn't look up. "That's a serious accusation."

"One that you're not denying," countered Jane harshly.

"Jane, that's enough," Clark chipped in, keen not to upset their meal ticket.

"While working with the natives they heard tales of a lost civilization in the heart of the jungle," Greystoke said slowly, as if marshaling his thoughts. "Stories told of a place of magnificent mineral wealth. As part of their good work"—he spat the word "good" out—"they tried working with the government, what was left of it at the time, thinking that they could convince the greedy junta not to exploit the wealth, but to preserve the environment. Of course, nobody was interested in that, and the city of Opar remained a mystery. Although," his voice dropped thoughtfully, "they were both convinced they knew where Opar was." He was silent for a long moment. "The Mbuti called the city a haunted place."

The words fell flat in the mist. All day the group hadn't managed to shake the feeling that somebody was watching their every step. A couple of times Robbie had doubled back along their path to try and catch their tail, but to no avail. On two occasions, Clark had pushed into the bush where they thought they'd detected movement, but found no signs of anybody passing through. It was as if a ghost was tracking them, and now, in the chill night, Greystoke's words had added menace.

Archie's disbelieving snigger cut through the night. "I think we've had our share of ghosts out here. We thought our camp was haunted, until Tarzan showed up."

Greystoke shook his head. "In my experience, there are still many things on this earth that remain unexplained. Opar is one of them. If it really does exist, we don't know which civilization built it, or what happened to them. There are legends . . . terrible tales about the people of Opar."

Robbie was enthralled despite himself. He asked in a low hush, "What kind of tales?"

Greystoke looked thoughtful for a moment, recalling the list of terrors he had heard about. "People who were not quite human. Mutations . . . hybrids . . . things that should not be. Bloodthirsty too. Many stories recount villages being attacked, the inhabitants whisked away. Devoured by the Opar's cannibalistic population."

Silence fell once again. Greystoke sniffed the fruit in his hands suspiciously and then bit into it. He let out a gasp of pleasure and smiled. "Incredible! It's like an explosion across my taste buds. I've never tasted such a thing!" he exclaimed.

Nobody paid any attention. They were all staring over his shoulder, hands frozen midway to their mouths. Greystoke suddenly turned, a chill running through him. A figure stood watching them from the trees. The mist diffused its outline and obscured features, but it looked almost childlike and remained motionless.

Greystoke shot a look at the others before slowly turning and standing.

"You must be Tarzan, I assume? Hello. I'm your cousin William."

The figure remained silent and Greystoke's uneasiness increased. He glanced at the others for encouragement, but they all remained motionless. Greystoke gathered himself, refusing to display any trace of fear.

"Don't be alarmed. We mean you no harm. You should recognize your friends here," he indicated to the others, partially turning as he did so. When he looked back the figure had gone. He blinked in surprise, his voice lowering to a raspy whisper. "Where'd he go?"

"He just vanished," whispered Robbie who had been watching the figure the whole time. "Like the fog just swallowed him up."

"And that wasn't Tarzan," Jane added.

"She's right," said Clark, keeping his voice low. "He's much bigger. And not the kinda bloke to be so shy."

The color drained from William Greystoke's face and he took a step away from where the figure had been.

Archie insisted they keep watch throughout the night. Despite their exhaustion, it took them all a long time to drift into a deep, dreamless sleep.

• • •

Some primal instinct woke Jane in the dead of the night. The campfire had faded to embers and her father was slumped asleep, still sitting upright, his head lolled on his chest. What had woken her? Instinct told her not to move. Her eyes rapidly adjusted to the darkness.

And then she saw movement. A single squat figure stepped out of the trees, a hunting spear in one hand. His footfalls were silent, like a phantom. The closer he got, the more unusual he looked. It was the same figure they had seen in the mist. Although he had the stature of a child, he had the wrinkled face of an old man. More figures appeared from the trees and Jane couldn't stop a startled gasp spilling from her lips. She moved to sit up, but felt a gentle pressure press her in place, and heard Clark's low voice as just the faintest of whispers.

"Don't."

The figure stopped, looking directly at Jane and Clark. There was no use pretending to sleep now. Jane sat up, and called clearly out.

"Who are you? What d'you want?"

Archie woke with a snort, his hand going for the rifle near his feet, but he froze when he saw the dozen figures surrounding them, none bigger than four feet in height, wearing crude garments and wielding primitive spears and bows with arrows notched.

"Pygmies," said Greystoke who had just bolted upright, waking Robbie. "We must be on their land."

Jane felt icy shards of fear trickle down the back of her neck as she recalled Greystoke's horrific tales of cannibals. The lead pygmy stepped forward, his face an unwelcoming grimace.

6

Even Tarzan found keeping up with the Targarni tough work. The apes carried the unconscious humans on their backs and galloped across the jungle floor with surprising speed. Goyad led the way, leaving the heavy work to his underlings. Thunder Mountain's steep incline did little to slow them, and the moonless night meant they blended into the jungle with ease.

From the lofty trees, Tarzan relied on scent and sound to follow the Targarni. Without a moon to light his way, even the trees could prove perilous for the ape-man. His keen eyesight was at its limits. Once in a while he caught sight of the ghostly Goyad below, but then the albino would be lost in the shadows. Occasionally, a swarm of fireflies glowed a green hue as the Targarni disturbed them, the only other visual cue Tarzan had.

There was no doubt they were heading back to their lair, but why? He had seen Targarni hunt game before. Unlike his own Mangani family, they relished the taste of flesh in the same way he did. So why did they need live prisoners? As he dwelled on these thoughts, he became determined to thwart the apes' plans. Not to save the lives of the prisoners, who would no doubt find other ways to die in the jungle, but to anger Goyad.

Eventually the relentless pace grew to be too much for the Targarni and they were forced to stop. They chose the banks of a fast-flowing stream that ran down the side of the mountain, stepping down in waterfalls every hundred feet. The trees gave way to a stretch of rocks where the Targarni dumped their captives and drank from the dark water.

Tarzan was grateful for the respite and gently lowered himself to the jungle floor so he could get a better look at the state of the three prisoners. They didn't stir. Tarzan crouched so low his chest slid across the cool rocks as he crawled closer.

Goyad's head shot up. Tarzan couldn't see his face, but he was certain the ape was looking in his direction. Surely he hadn't been detected? The crashing waterfall masked his movements and as he was downwind of the Targarni, they couldn't pick up his scent. The white ape didn't move for several long moments before turning back around and lapping water from the stream.

Tarzan edged closer to the captives so they were almost within arm's reach. He positioned himself behind a smooth boulder that would provide ample cover if the apes chose to look up again.

He suddenly heard a sharp intake of breath from the male prisoner. Tarzan recoiled into the shadows as the man groaned and sat up, clutching his head. He said something to the other two prone figures, but they were unconscious. There was not enough light for the man to take in his surroundings, and he hadn't yet seen the dark shadows of the Targarni against the deeper black of the jungle.

Before his eyes could adjust to the dark, Goyad raced across with two powerful bounds, his jaws stretched wide as he howled. For a lesser mortal than Tarzan, the sight of the ghostly ape was enough to freeze the blood. The man was rooted to the spot as Goyad's powerful fist clobbered him across the head, knocking him unconscious again. The albino inspected the man for a moment, then, satisfied his prey was still alive, he returned to the stream.

The cold, calculating attack impressed Tarzan, who remained motionless just a yard away. The Targarni soon finished their rest and three chimps hoisted the prisoners over their backs before they continued.

Tarzan did not immediately move from his hiding place. It would be folly to further pursue Goyad in the dark; he knew exactly where the apes were heading. What value the prisoners had, he didn't know, but it was enough to warrant keeping them alive. Not so long ago, Tarzan would have recklessly pursued the Targarni, if only to provoke and annoy them, but now he felt the weight of responsibility toward his family. He had led them here, and while the Targarni were around, he couldn't risk getting injured or worse. The Mangani needed him, and so Goyad should wait.

However, Tarzan's unquenchable curiosity was getting the better of him.

• • •

The pygmies surrounded Greystoke's party: expressions fierce, weapons raised. The lead figure eyed Greystoke and his companions with hostility. He walked in an arc around Jane, his eyes studying her ruffled blonde hair. She had seen that air of curiosity before with Tarzan; blonde was not a natural shade in the heart of the jungle. The pygmy's skin was a natural dark brown, camouflaged further by the dried mud he wore as war paint. His face was most definitely that of a man in his forties, but he barely came up to Jane's shoulders, and she was by no means tall. The tip of the spear moved closer toward her, and it took all her courage not to flinch. The stone blade lifted her hair, then let it fall back to her shoulders.

Lord Greystoke suddenly said something in an unfamiliar language. The pygmies' eyes widened as they recognized their own tongue and replied rapidly.

"You speak their language?" said Archie in surprise.

"A little," said Greystoke, his face screwed in concentration as he tried to decipher what was being said. "They're Mbuti people. . . . Or a tribe of them. They're speaking Bantu. . . . But the dialect is not one I've heard before. There are some similarities. . . ."

Clark snorted. "Glad you're such an expert."

"There are over a hundred and forty dialects in use," said Greystoke tartly, without taking his eyes off the lead pygmy who was now gesturing with his spear. "Even out here, there are clans who seldom need to have contact with the outside world. I think they are claiming this is their territory." The leader gestured angrily to the trees. "As far as I can tell, they have been forced from their own lands. Forced out here."

"They look happy 'bout it too," said Clark.

"Forced?" said Jane. "Who'd do that to them?"

Greystoke relayed the question and the leader snapped back a reply, gesturing to the Westerners.

"It appears I did," said Greystoke, carefully keeping his face neutral.

Jane glanced at Robbie, who was thinking the same thing. "Do they know who you are?" she asked carefully.

"If they did, I would be dead already." Greystoke glanced at her and Robbie. "Thinking of turning me in?"

"It crossed my mind," said Robbie grimly.

Greystoke forced a smile on his face. "Then you would lose your meal ticket. And your own lives. They are not indiscriminate killers, but they will fight for what they believe is theirs. And they see no distinction between you and me."

He spoke in a halting dialect to the pygmies, gesturing to himself and the others. The exchange continued for some minutes before the leader finally cast the group a grim look, then disappeared back into the forest. When Jane looked around, the other pygmies had silently vanished too.

Greystoke finally let out the pent-up breath he'd been holding. His smile dropped, replaced by concerned furrows across his forehead. "I explained we were just passing through to try and convince the people who took their land to return it. They're going to escort us most of the way." He studied the dark trees; there was no sign of the forest people.

"So you lied to them?" said Jane caustically. "Pretended to be somebody else?"

Greystoke shrugged and returned to his tent, pausing before he climbed in to look steadily at Jane. "I saved your life. You're most welcome." He climbed into the tent, zipping the flap up without waiting for a reply.

Archie looked to where he suspected the pygmies were watching them. "Well I suppose that means we're safe for the night. I suggest we rest. I know I need it." He returned to his tent, yawning loudly.

Clark limped over to Jane, who still stood her ground. He spoke low, watching as Robbie returned to his own tent. "Listen, Jane. We don't often see eye to eye, but you gotta stop being so pigheaded and keep your *bek* shut. We got a good thing goin' with his lordship, and now it seems like Tarzan is down on his list of priorities, so what have you got to worry 'bout?"

"It doesn't mean I have to like him."

"Nah, you don't. He's a pompous *rooinek.*" His South African accent became more pronounced with the Afrikaans slang. "His heart may be in the wrong place, but his wallet ain't. We need this"—Jane opened her mouth to speak but Clark raised a finger to silence her—"an' if you don't, your dad does. It's your mother's fault you're out here in the first place; don't let it be your fault he's gotta stay."

Jane felt a stab of guilt. She knew that was exactly the reaction Clark was aiming for, but it still hurt. He limped back to his tent, and Jane swore he was deliberately making his injury more pronounced to make her feel bad. Again, the sickening feeling of guilt: a feeling that would keep her awake long into the night.

• • •

The mist lingered on into the following morning, but as they broke camp and pressed on down the mountain, it slowly lifted. They were all hungry and tired. Greystoke had hoped the forest people would return their stolen food, but their enigmatic escorts remained unseen, although the group could easily feel their eyes on them every step of the way.

By lunchtime, they made it to the base of the mountain range where the trees thinned out to a small grass plain, just a few miles across. Greystoke's pace increased as he entered a code into the GPS.

"There should be a river, this way. We'll be picked up there," he said, indicating a spot located an angle away from their current position.

The brown grass was almost as tall as they were, making it impossible to see ahead. Only the rising jungle-clad mountains lining the valley provided a point of reference; otherwise they could have been walking in circles without realizing it. Robbie noticed that Jane had become increasingly concerned since they stepped into the grassland. He was sure the pygmies were not following them any longer. However, Jane's head kept snapping up at every sound she heard.

"What's the matter?" Robbie asked Jane, catching her up as Archie and Greystoke led the way, batting aside napier grass.

"I've been here before," she answered with a tremor in her voice. Before she could go on, there was a shout from Greystoke.

"Stop!" he yelled.

Jane froze, looking around sharply for danger. But Greystoke laughed loudly. "This is it!" he said, pointing.

The grass abruptly gave way to the red-soil banks of a murky brown river that meandered through the plains. The river was twenty yards wide and moved sluggishly, but the adventurers knew what dangers could lurk in the water, and kept their distance. Greystoke found a large rock and sat down with a sigh.

Clark looked around. "Now what?"

"We wait," said Greystoke. "Shouldn't be too long."

A crack in the grass got everybody's attention. Greystoke waved his hand dismissively.

"The pygmies. No doubt ensuring we leave their land."

Everybody visibly relaxed, except Jane who kept looking around. Her skittishness was unnerving to Robbie, who had grown to trust her instincts in the wild. He tried to ignore her, but she was too distracting. Luckily, Archie broke the atmosphere as he skipped stones across the river.

"So why did you move the pygmies off their land?" he asked as casually as he could.

"They were in the way," said Greystoke simply. "No offense to them. In fact, we employ any who wish to work for us."

Archie threw another stone, sending ripples across the brown surface. He fished one more stone from the muddy bank, inching closer to the water.

"Dad, careful . . ." said Jane as his next stone bounced three times across the still surface.

Greystoke continued, oblivious to how close Archie had moved toward the river. "Lets them afford a better standard of life than our primitive jungle friends enjoy."

Archie turned around, his eyes searching Greystoke for answers. "But it's their land, isn't it?" Clark nudged his friend. The meaning was clear: Don't argue until Greystoke pays up.

"Dad . . ." Jane's warning went unheeded.

Greystoke sniggered. "Who owns anything out here? They have no idea what this land is really worth."

A deep roar and sudden flurry of movement—not from the water, but from the grass—as a flash of tawny fur landed on Greystoke, pitching him off the rock and rolling through the red dirt. It was a huge maned lion. His claws dug into Greystoke's back, drawing blood as it pinned him down. The lion roared, so loud and sonorous that Robbie felt his ribcage shake.

Clark fumbled for his sidearm. Staggering backward, he lost his balance, and dropped to his backside. His gun skittered away. He groped for it, but Jane darted forward and kicked it farther out of reach.

"NO!" she screamed. "You'll just annoy him!"

The lion turned toward her and snarled, his mouth extending wide enough to encompass Greystoke's head and shoulders. He was a massive specimen. Greystoke gibbered, tears rolling down his cheeks. Jane took a step forward, her hands raised out in front of her.

"Easy! It's me. Remember Tarzan?"

Now Robbie understood. The last time they had seen lions

was when Tarzan had rescued them from Tafari's camp. Then he had been riding a lion as if it were a domesticated steed. Was this Numa? Tarzan's friend? It was certainly *a* Numa—Robbie was still uncertain how Tarzan named the creatures around him.

Jane bravely stepped closer and the lion roared again. Even several yards away, Robbie could smell his meaty breath.

"Numa. I'm a friend. Friend," said Jane as she approached, then did something contrary to all common sense. She knelt down so that Numa towered over her.

"Jane!" hissed Robbie. "Don't."

Numa pressed a paw harder against Greystoke's back, as if kneading him. The Englishman whimpered in pain. Then Numa removed his paw and took a step toward Jane. She didn't flinch, and maintained eye contact as the beast pressed close, sniffing her.

Robbie held his breath. He saw Archie and Clark were rigid with fear, hoping Jane knew what she was doing. Robbie guessed she was just as terrified.

The lion growled. It was as if an engine was idling close to Jane's head. Numa's breath blew her hair. Then, the aggressive sounds suddenly turned to a distinctive purr. He rubbed the side of his massive head against Jane, marking his scent.

Jane giggled with relief, and scratched Numa's head, her fingers digging deep into the flea-ridden fur, and Numa purred more contently as he paced around her. She stood, wobbling as the lion playfully jostled her.

"I think he remembers me," she said with a broad smile.

Robbie slowly moved and the lion growled a warning. "I don't think he knows me," said Robbie who had never been so close to a lion. Archie and Clark remained motionless.

"Can you tell him to go away?" said Archie, his gaze switching to Greystoke who was still bleeding, though his wounds didn't look so bad.

"Well, we are on *his* land," said Jane giving Greystoke a meaningful look.

Robbie caught a flicker of movement in the grass—was it one of the Mbuti? Numa caught it too, but before Numa could react, a boom echoed across the valley as a huge helicopter swooped into it at high speed. The enclosing mountains reverberated the sound into a terrifying roar.

Numa bellowed, roaring fiercely, but backed into the grass. He knew better than to take on the forces of modern man. With a final roar, he vanished into the grassland.

The chopper circled around before hovering over them. The rotor's downdraft pressed the grass flat, kicking up dry debris into a whirlwind. Robbie crouched as the helicopter landed on the riverbank. He was forced to close his eyes to avoid the whirling dust, but not before noting the stylized Greystoke logo on the side of the machine. For the first time, he began to wonder just what resources Greystoke had at his disposal.

7

The opening between the lion's paws was bathed in darkness, and Tarzan didn't have enough light to make out any detail inside. He paused at the entrance, his keen senses alert to everything. The wind had changed direction, and the air now tasted unpleasant, like rotten eggs. Through the black mask of the jungle, he could see flecks of glowing red rock spitting from the cone of the volcano above. The wind carried a faint, constant rumble that made him anxious.

He turned his attention back to the cave. The stench of decay from within was stronger than ever, but he could still detect the scent of the Targarni and their captives, even if he couldn't see into the void. The dark offered no terrors for the ape-man, but walking blind was not something he relished either.

A few careful paces into the cave revealed stone steps leading down. He guessed they were man-made, but couldn't see anything. Through touch alone he discovered the crumbling stone had been worn smooth by passing feet and running water. Several steps down he glanced back to the entrance, his eyes adjusting to the subtle shades of darkness beyond the entrance.

As his eyes grew accustomed to the tunnel, Tarzan became aware of a faint glow. At first he thought it was his eyes playing a trick on him, but after several minutes, he grew accustomed to a faint green light clinging to the walls and ceiling. Closer inspection revealed it was some type of moss. He carefully continued down and the tunnel around him grew lighter, filled with soft luminescence.

The steps turned in a graceful bend and the tunnel widened. A cool breeze blew Tarzan's shoulder-length hair, and it seemed to increase with each passing step. Carried with it was an increasing scent of Targarni. Still he descended and it grew warmer. Tarzan judged he must be well under the slopes of Thunder Mountain. He pressed on until another jink in the passage revealed a stronger light ahead and a faint roar.

The tunnel came to a halt and Tarzan froze in the opening as he gazed beyond at a huge cavern. Green and blue bioluminescent fungus clung to the walls and ceiling in long trails that made it seem as if the stars had leaked underground. It was much brighter there, so much so that Tarzan could easily see across the cave.

Massive rock spires stretched from floor to ceiling some hundred feet above. The roof was a mass of slender stalactites—most much longer than the ape-man—through which flocks of bats raced at high speeds. The floor sported matching stalagmites, but most had been cleared to provide a thoroughfare across the cave to another tunnel. The opening to this one was some twenty feet in diameter and circular, crafted in stone to look like the mouth of a giant beast. The fangs were blunt from age, and the features worn to nothing more than a faint trace, but it must have once been a fearsome image. A pair of small lakes sat at either end of the cavern. Their surfaces were motionless, but Tarzan swore he saw something large move below the crystal-clear surface of one.

What impressed Tarzan most was the slender stone bridge that cut across the middle of the cavern. It was the width of a man, forcing creatures to cross in single file. Tarzan stood on it and gazed down. It spanned a whitewater river that cut through the rock a couple of feet below, appearing from one narrow cave and vanishing through another. The pale luminescence from the walls made

the spume glow as it struck jagged rocks. There was no doubt—
escape would be impossible for anybody unfortunate enough to fall
in. Tarzan could see the lake connected to the river and guessed the
water avenues were all connected in a gigantic network.

Above the noise of the river, he heard a faint scream followed
by shouting. The Targarni's female prisoner was awake. Tarzan
sprinted across the bridge and raced through the open maw of the
stone beast, deeper into the unknown sanctuary.

• • •

Jane's stomach lurched as the helicopter banked sharply left, following the path of the meandering river with reckless speed. The
jungle below was an unfamiliar blur. Robbie clung on to a handle
mounted just above the door and was grinning like a fool as the
chopper suddenly banked right.

Archie and Clark sat in flight seats opposite and didn't say anything, although Jane suspected her father was enjoying the ride too.
She hated it and was fully aware that Greystoke was taking them
far deeper into the jungle, away from their camp. Without any rec-
ognizable landmarks, it would prove very difficult to return home
in a hurry. Where Greystoke had previously relied on the loggers,
the balance of power had now firmly shifted in his favor. Jane wondered if the others had realized that yet. Until they did, she would
have to continue quietly sabotaging Greystoke's plans.

Greystoke sat in the copilot's seat and hadn't said a word to them
since they'd taken off. The pilot had tended to his wounds, which
proved to be nothing more severe than shallow cuts. Fortunately
for Greystoke, Numa had been in a playful mood.

Jane heard a crackle in the headset she was wearing to minimize
the rotor noise. Greystoke's voice filtered through. "We're almost
there. Get ready for landing."

Jane was unsure how to get ready, and the quizzical look of the
others showed they were thinking the same thing. The chopper suddenly rose, causing Jane's stomach to plummet as they climbed up
the steep banks of a mountain. The jungle canopy was closer than

ever and she couldn't shake the thought that the pilot was going to crash. But he was skillful, and pivoted the helicopter over the gray shards of stone that poked from the mountaintop and revealed the vista beyond. Jane craned to get a better view through the cockpit canopy between Archie and Clark. What she saw made her heart sink.

A huge swathe of jungle had been cleared for several miles, exposing the red clay beneath like an ugly scar in the landscape. The ground was laced with dirty brown streams that fed polluted water back into the rivers, and everywhere she looked bulldozers and excavators tracked to and fro, open-pit mining the landscape. Clark peered through the window as they flew over the site, impressed at the scale of the operation. A couple of boats and a floatplane were moored on the river, adjacent to a pair of large metal fuel tanks. It seemed as if Greystoke had everything he needed to stay in the wilderness.

The helicopter pivoted over a landing pad, nothing more than a slab of concrete set into the mud a hundred feet from a set of portable cabins that fanned out across the site like a shantytown. The scale was greater than Karibu Mji and the devastation was above and beyond anything they had achieved even after months of logging.

They landed so smoothly that Jane didn't feel a thing. The rotors quickly wound down and a pair of ground crew rushed over to help Greystoke out. They kept their heads bent down as they passed under the slow-spinning rotor blades, despite the fact that there was more than enough clearance.

The side door cranked open and the ground crew gestured for them to exit. One of the crewmembers wore a perfectly white shirt that looked out of place in the dirty mine around them; he looked like the poster boy for a corporation with more cash than morals. He walked ahead with Greystoke, and the group caught the name Edward from a snatch of conversation. The other was a woman with flame-red hair. She didn't look happy to see them, but was apparently under orders to be hospitable.

"Welcome," she said with an Australian accent.

The smell of dust and diesel struck Jane. Every breath she took tasted of dirt. "What are you mining?" she asked. The woman ignored her and helped Archie, who grinned at her with all the charm he could muster, out of the helicopter.

"An absolute pleasure. Lovely to meet you. I'm Archie."

"Idra," acknowledged the woman.

Jane rolled her eyes and hurried over to Greystoke and Edward. Greystoke was gesticulating, his voice raised: "Don't let any more of those damned pygmies in here. How hard can that be?" He shot a scathing look in the direction of a dozen barefoot Mbuti men carrying heavy machinery. Unlike the people they had encountered in the jungle, the men wore grubby Westernized clothing and their faces bore a pale unsmiling mask. Jane thought they looked more like slaves than workers.

"What are you mining here?" she asked, pushing herself between Greystoke and Edward and looking around. She noticed Archie was still chatting to a bored-looking Idra as Robbie and Clark took in the site, Clark occasionally pointing to huge pieces of digging machinery.

Greystoke hesitated, obviously not used to being spoken to so casually in front of staff. He shot Edward a look before answering. "Coltan."

"Never heard of it," said Jane crossing her arms and turning to face him. "I guess it's pretty valuable, otherwise you wouldn't be poisoning the land?"

Edward raised his hand and smoothly moved in between them, a job he was no doubt amply paid for. "This is a fully legal operation we have out here, miss."

His tone irritated Jane, but she didn't let it show. Instead she forced a smile. "That's not what I asked, *Edward.*"

Greystoke nudged his spokesman aside. "Coltan is very valuable and we need it," he said primly. "You use it all the time, everybody does. In your phone, car ignition systems, lights, computers—just about every electrical item uses coltan, and it just so happens that one of the world's largest supplies is under this jungle."

"So you'll rip up the rainforest just to find it?"

"Ah, now you're a flag-waving eco-warrior are you? Spend a few months in this hellhole and you think it should all be preserved?"

"I've only just got here and I can see what you're doing is wrong."

Greystoke laughed, his eyes narrowing. "Oh, the irony of such a statement coming from the daughter of a logger." He shook his head condescendingly.

Jane tensed, ready for an argument, but Archie and Clark caught up with them.

"Nice operation," said Clark casually. Greystoke didn't see the look he shot at Jane. It spoke volumes: Shut up. "You must extract a lot of ore from here."

Greystoke sniffed at the idea and walked toward the cabins, forcing the others to keep pace with him. "It used to be a lucrative mine. My father set it up on the assumption the coltan reserves ran deep. Alas, he was mistaken. We've taken about all we can from this area."

"Is that why you wanted the survey plans from the airplane?" said Robbie suddenly. "You think whatever's in the lost city of Opar is worth more than this?"

As he reached the cabin, Greystoke spun on his heel and glared at Robbie with deep-rooted annoyance. "Much more! But those plans alone cover a huge geographic survey of the region. My uncle spent millions surveying this land." He waved his hand toward the jungle. "And with thousands of square miles still unexplored. Who knows what's out there, waiting for us? An inconceivable fortune . . ."

"And it's all yours?" said Jane sarcastically.

Greystoke opened the door of a cabin, pausing only to look back at her. "It is there for whoever takes it first," he said with a sardonic smile. "Survival of the fittest."

. . .

Deep underground, Tarzan sprinted along a straight tunnel that angled further down, following the sound of screaming. The temperature was increasing and sweat glistened on his skin. It was more cloying than the humid rainforest above, a dry unforgiving heat.

A light ahead burned with more ferocity than the luminous vegetation clinging to the walls. Tarzan slowed his pace, dropping to all fours and pressing himself against the smooth stone as he approached the opening.

There was a bigger cavern beyond, and the tunnel Tarzan was in offered a view from midway up. It was a colossal natural cavern. Steps led down to the massive floor below, carved from the stone by hand. Several single-story buildings, now nothing more than ruins, spread across the floor in what would have once been a subterranean town. Luminous lichen and half-moon fungi clung to the rubble wherever it could, giving an almost dreamlike quality.

In a wide area, like a town plaza, the Targarni had gathered—more of them than Tarzan had ever seen before. They were pale from spending too much time underground, but none as pure white as Goyad, who stood on his knuckles on an elevated platform. The apes appeared to be watching the captives. Tarzan could not see the humans as the few buildings remaining standing blocked his view. But he could hear the female's screams.

He edged closer to the top of the staircase. If he were seen, only his head start would prevent him from being torn limb from limb. Almost nothing frightened Tarzan, yet the thought of fighting an inevitable losing battle with the apes made him cautious. The steps fanned out in a graceful one hundred and eighty degrees, allowing Tarzan to edge down the side flanks, which offered better cover from prying eyes. Luckily, the Targarni's interest was focused on Goyad.

A quarter of the way down the steps, Tarzan was able to see around the buildings. Most of the light came from a pair of massive stone bowls standing on plinths, etched in strange pictorial symbols. He could only just see the tongues of flames licking over the edges. The flames provided dramatic under-lighting to a thirty-foot-tall pair of coiling snakes looming over the bowls, carved out of stone, their mouths open, ready to strike and revealing black stone fangs. Their features were harsh and finely detailed, unlike the carvings near the entrance, which had been dulled by time and weather. The snake's eyes seemed to sparkle with living malice.

Tarzan's gaze was dragged back down to the scene unfolding at the base of the snake's mighty stone coils. Two of the human captives lay on a massive slab of stone—the female and the man who had been struck by Goyad. Where the third was, Tarzan could not see; perhaps he was too late to save him. Narrow stone blocks across their hands and legs restrained the man and woman. The female struggled, but the man was still unconscious. Tarzan frowned, wondering what Goyad's intentions were. He placed a hand on the step below, intending to lower himself to the cavern floor—but froze suddenly as another figure appeared at the altar.

It was a woman, tall and slender with long dark hair adorned with luminous specks of lichen. She wore a long robe that looked as if it had been fashioned from many other garments. From this distance he couldn't guess her age, but she moved with utter confidence amongst the Targarni, who seemed to consider her one of their own. She waved her arms over the victims and spoke aloud, her words unintelligible as they echoed around the cavern. Whatever was said drove the apes into a cacophony of wild hooting that rumbled across the broken city.

The woman retrieved a metal sword from the floor. Even in the dim light the polished blade gleamed. She held it above the female captive who screamed louder than ever.

Tarzan was transfixed by the spectacle as the robed woman brought the blade down across the unconscious man's throat. The sight didn't phase the ape-man in the least—he had done far worse with his bare hands—but the captive woman's wailing rose in angst as she was splattered with blood.

Tarzan enjoyed eating raw meat, but something inside him had always cautioned him not to eat ape or human flesh. Instead he satisfied himself on the animals he found foraging in the jungle. Still, even knowing the value of fresh meat, Tarzan was surprised when the robed woman cast the man's severed limbs into the yowling mob of Targarni. The apes shrieked with bloodlust as they scrambled for the tastier morsels, causing waves of motion in the crowd.

Tarzan felt his stomach knot; some deep primal instinct told him this was wrong.

The woman was saving the tender internal organs for herself and Goyad. Tarzan knew that if he hesitated any further, the female prisoner would be their next kill. He had no intention of letting Goyad or the strange woman have any further barbaric enjoyment.

Tarzan quickly descended the steps and, hunched low, ran to the cover offered by the ruins. A cautious glance assured him that the Targarni were still indulging in their feast and none was looking in his direction. The robed woman had almost finished her macabre act and Tarzan sensed it wouldn't be long before she turned on the female. He had to work out a way around the mass of apes. His gaze followed the rough natural cave wall up as it curved toward the giant snake statues. The gap was wide, but he was sure he could make the leap between them.

With agility honed over a lifetime, Tarzan scampered up the wall. His feet and fingers found uneven edges just wide enough to balance on. His toned muscles pulled him higher and higher. Never once did he consider what would happen if he fell—that had never happened before and the idea had never crossed his mind. In no time at all he had reached a narrow ledge some forty feet up. It provided just enough purchase for him to crouch tightly. He sprang into the void.

The Targarni below had no reason to look up; instead they were following the blade in the woman's hand as it danced over the female captive. The apes howled in anticipation of the feast, some baring blood-coated fangs in rictus grins. They didn't see Tarzan land on the curved stone body of one of the statues. His feet slipped on the smooth surface and for a moment he was in danger of sliding off and dropping into the throng. With honed reflexes, Tarzan's hand shot out and grabbed the carved crest that ran the length of the snake. His feet cycled in the air, but his single-handed hold prevented him from falling. With every sinew tensed, Tarzan pulled himself up, planting his feet firmly on the statue's curves.

With his free hand he snatched the vine rope from his waist and swung the lassoed end up to the flaming bowl, snagging it on one of the ornate carvings on the plinth that supported it. The loose end he tied around his waist with a simple knot. His mind had already plotted the route he needed to take, so he didn't have to think. He braced himself against one snake, then leaped across and down to the opposite statue. With minimal effort, Tarzan zigzagged his way down between the statues as the robed woman lifted the sword. In the same moment, she looked up. The dazed, almost sleepy expression on her face suddenly transformed into absolute shock as she saw the wild man bear down on her.

Tarzan landed just behind the woman, shouldering her into Goyad just as the ape recognized Tarzan. With a grunt, Tarzan lifted the stone block from across the captive female's hands. It was surprisingly heavy, and he had to brace himself to fully lift it aside. It was covered in intricate carvings, which were in turn covered in long-dried blood. He noticed two hollows had been carved from the block, designed to perfectly restrain the victim's wrists. He hauled the female over his shoulder and spun to face the riled Targarni, who were only just recovering from the unexpected rescue and waiting for a cue to attack.

Tarzan faced the horde and bellowed the deep challenge of a male bull ape. It was enough to make the apes pause—and it gave Tarzan enough time to yank the rope fastened around his waist. With a mighty rumble, the flaming bowl started to topple from the plinth. Tarzan had caused hell to rain down into the cavern.

8

Albert Werper leaned on the table with one hand, the other carefully tracing a finger over the detailed geo-survey maps Lord Greystoke had retrieved from the plane wreck. Greystoke's archeologist lifted a magnifying glass and leaned closer, examining a contour and double-checking the maps' color-coded legend. He breathed through his narrow nose, so his nostrils flared and whistled every time he came across an interesting feature.

After examining the maps for close to thirty minutes, he stood up, his back cricking as he stretched. Then he scratched his scalp, the brown curls now damp with sweat and flat against his skull. He didn't look at the other occupants in the room, but stared dreamily into space.

"Well?" Lord Greystoke prompted. He sat in the corner of the modern cabin, logging details of his previous adventures on a rugged laptop. The site nurse had treated his wounds and declared him to be fit, though he had insisted on bandages being wrapped around his midriff and wore his shirt open, sporting the bandages as a brave war wound.

Werper watched Archie and Clark, who sat at one table finishing a meal. Jane was asleep in a chair, her head slumped awkwardly on the arm. Robbie slouched in another corner, watching Werper intently. The moment he had met the man, he disliked him. Albert Werper was ferrety, his eyes constantly shifting, never focusing on the person he was talking to. When he spoke, it was often curtly, as if he had more important people to speak to. Even with Greystoke he was often snappy and aloof, but the English lord gave no outward indication that he was annoyed. Greystoke had introduced him as an archeologist, but said little more.

Greystoke sighed, and snapped the laptop's lid down with a thud to get Werper's attention. "Are they of use?"

Werper nodded, then paused. "No, there's a problem," he suddenly countered.

"They are my uncle's maps, correct?"

Werper paced the room, gazing thoughtfully through the window. "Yes . . . Well, you found them on their plane, didn't you? I hardly think there's room for duplicity here. They're very accurate, marvelous detail." He paused again, internally working through the problems.

"So . . . ?" Greystoke prompted warily.

"So the landscape is intricately recorded—rock strata, rivers . . . even coltan deposits." Werper's eyes narrowed mockingly when he saw Greystoke get excited. "But there are no markers, no features we can readily identify. They could be maps of any jungle in the world."

Robbie smiled inwardly, careful not to look at Clark who made a disappointed huffing sound. Annoyance flashed across Greystoke's face and he crossed to the map, studying it intently.

Werper didn't turn around. "Oh, there are ruins marked on the map. Opar, I can only presume. What other civilization could have created them?"

Greystoke found the ruins marked on the map—nothing more than three tiny squares. A handwritten legend across the area read "Savage Lands" in small letters. "So these mountain ridges, valleys—all we have to do is transpose them over the maps we have. Surely that will reveal the location?"

"We have satellite imagery, but nothing showing these contours. Nothing this accurate."

Robbie allowed himself to relax a little as Greystoke grew increasingly frustrated. With luck, this whole venture would turn out to be nothing more than a wild goose chase and they could return back to the camp, leaving Tarzan at peace. During his time spent with the ape-man, Robbie discovered an affinity with him. His life had been in Tarzan's hands so many times, yet the wild man had asked for nothing in return. . . . Unlike almost everybody else Robbie had encountered in the past.

"There are rivers here," said Greystoke persistently. Clark rose and limped across to look at the map.

Werper's laugh contained no humor. "Do you know how many rivers are out there? Most haven't even been mapped. This is a fool's errand, Bill." Greystoke flinched at the common use of his name. Werper didn't care; his temper was rising. "Do you know what it's like to be this close to something you've searched for all your life"— he held up his thumb and forefinger fractionally apart—"only to have it tease you? Prove impossible to achieve?" His hands bunched into fists and it looked like he wanted to punch something, but was too timid to try. "Maybe . . . maybe it's all wrong. Maybe Opar is nothing more than a Mbuti myth."

"Then why mark it on a map?" said Greystoke. "My uncle was not prone to flights of fancy. I have never met a more boring man!"

"What's so special about Opar?" said Robbie as casually as he could, but inwardly his curiosity about uncovering lost riches was burning. "It's just some old city. You always hear about lost treasure—it never turns out to be true."

Werper spun around, giving Robbie the full power of his piercing blue eyes. He suddenly became animated, hands gesticulating as he spoke. Robbie was unsure if it was passion or madness.

"This is not just some lost city. This is a civilization that fell through the cracks of history. As big as the Mayans, as mighty as the Egyptian pharaohs . . . now only a legend passed down verbally in pygmy culture. A city of untold riches run by a cannibalistic ruling clan who spilled more blood than the Aztecs, who worshipped animals as their gods. What happened to them? Why their mysterious decline?" Werper spread his arms out as if offering himself to the Oparian gods. "If I was the one to uncover a new civilization . . . my name would echo amongst the greats. . . ." His hands suddenly dropped to his side with sadness, his gaze becoming unfocused again. "If only we could find it. . . ."

Clark tapped the map. "What about this?"

Greystoke glanced at the tightly packed contour lines. "Mountains. There are plenty to choose from out there."

"I can see that," said Clark testily. The thought of any riches slipping through his fingers was galling. "But this curve 'ere. Doesn't it strike you as odd?" He traced a finger around a cylindrical edge.

Greystoke leaned over, his brow knitted. "Looks almost volcanic to me."

"A volcano . . ." mumbled Greystoke thoughtfully.

Robbie crossed to the map to get a better look. The mountain's contour lines were indeed distinctly circular.

Werper snorted. "Do you know how many volcanoes are out there? This whole region is a tectonic nightmare. There are eight known volcanoes in the Democratic Republic of the Congo alone, Nyamuragira being one of the most active on the planet. There could be eighty more out there, hidden by the jungle."

Clark shrugged and limped back to his seat. Greystoke continued studying the map, then noticed the smirk on Clark's face.

"What aren't you telling us?"

Clark enjoyed being the center of attention and picked at the food on his plate. He gave Archie a calculating look that clearly showed he had just worked out how to turn the situation to their advantage. Robbie began to feel his heart sink.

"Our deal was originally to unite you with your long-lost cousin."

"And that still stands, should we come across him," said Greystoke slowly.

"And I believe half the cut was mentioned for leading you to the aircraft, right?"

Greystoke stiffened slightly, turning his head to one side as his neck cracked. "I am a man of my word, Mr. Philander," said Greystoke with a cocky grin. By using Clark's real name, the one he hated, he'd subtly revealed he knew more about the loggers than he had let on. "Or do you prefer Samuel?" he teased. "So before you try to blackmail me, please remember your own position."

Clark's smug smile dropped and his eyes narrowed slightly. "If we help you find it, Archie and I deserve a cut at whatever's in Opar. Agreed?"

"A cut," said Greystoke carefully, exchanging a glance with Werper. "Agreed. But since we are laying down demands, here are mine. If you should try to renege on our deal, then I won't hesitate to expose you and your logging operation to government authorities." Clark and Archie exchanged worried glances. Lord Greystoke continued. "If we are in this, we are in it together. Agreed?"

The room fell quiet, save for the constant background thrum of excavating machinery outside. Werper had his back to the conversation and was poring over the map to see what he had missed. Robbie noticed Jane hadn't moved, but her eyes were half open as she listened.

"Agreed," said Clark as he climbed painfully to his feet to offer Lord Greystoke his hand. They solemnly shook. "Y'see, there is a volcano about a day or so away from where their plane crashed. She's been there." He nodded toward Jane. Robbie noticed her eyes were closed again. "An' I 'appen to know which way she went, with your cousin, no less."

Greystoke's eyes flicked between the map and Clark. Then he nodded. "It's worth a try. If you're right. . . ."

Clark held up his hand reassuringly. "I reckon I am right. So, let's talk numbers." He grinned like a shark.

•   •   •

Red-hot coals rained down across the howling Targarni as Tarzan heaved on his vine rope, pulling the huge flaming bowl off the slender stone plinth. The coals, huge chunks of black volcanic rock, came first, smashing to the ground in a fountain of sparks that singed the fur of the slower Targarni.

The robed woman stared at Tarzan in surprise, the sword clanging from her grip. Her eyes went wide and she staggered backward. Goyad leaped between them, teeth bared—which looked all the more terrifying due to the fresh blood smeared across his snout. There were only five yards between the two, and Tarzan knew his speed would be restricted with the weight of the female over his shoulder.

Goyad was ready to spring as the huge flaming bowl hit the ground with a terrible crack of stone on rock. Tarzan tensed, unable to judge which way the heavy stone would fall. His heart pounded and the floor under his feet trembled when the rim of the bowl sliced between them. Tarzan let out a snort of victory as the concave bowl rolled away from him, spilling a mass of flames toward Goyad. Blazing rocks burned patches of the ape's fur away to the pale skin beneath. He howled in pain and raced away from the flames spreading across the floor. With a powerful kick, the albino ape leaped for the sanctuary of a wall projecting from the nearest ruin.

The huge stone bowl continued rolling on its rim and Tarzan ran with it as it scythed through the lines of Targarni. They ignored Tarzan, more concerned about avoiding the fire or being crushed as the bowl steamrolled toward them. Tarzan saw several unfortunate Targarni fully ablaze, rolling on the floor screaming as they tried to quell the flames. He grinned—he couldn't have planned a more destructive revenge. Tarzan made it across the plaza and vaulted up the steps two at a time with ease, even with the female thrown over his shoulders.

Halfway up the steps the bowl finally teetered over. It managed one mighty grinding spin before thundering to a halt. By this time Tarzan was already in the cavern above and sprinting across the narrow stone bridge.

· · ·

The Targarni did not follow. Tarzan was panting heavily as he raced up the final steps between the lion's claws. He could not afford to rest now. Goyad might not have immediately given chase, but Tarzan was sure the ape and his cohorts would soon be scouring the area. He didn't see the point in testing his luck any further.

He checked the female he had saved. She had been unnaturally quiet during the escape and when he carefully laid her on the forest floor her head slumped to the side. Tarzan hoped she wasn't dead; other than annoying Goyad, that would have made his entire adventure a waste of time. But he did not know the woman, so if she lived or died Tarzan would accept that nature had chosen her path. There were few beings he cared for outside his tribe and, as he examined the woman, he was reminded it had been some days since he had last seen Jane. Moving to new feeding grounds with his family had been a necessity, and he only hoped Jane hadn't got into any trouble while he had been away. He tried to put that distraction from his mind as he focused his attention on the woman.

He felt a pulse in her neck; it was slow but strong. She must have passed out from sheer terror at the thought of what was about to happen to her. Her hair was black, her skin darker than Tarzan's own, and she wore the familiar khaki uniform most jungle explorers chose. As far as he could judge, she was older than Jane, but not by much.

Tarzan listened for any signs of pursuit, but only the jungle's twilight chorus could be heard. The sky was already growing dark, and the first stars appeared in the deep blue, shining their ancient light. But there was another glow to the air, a tinge of red reflecting from the few clouds. And now that he was listening for it, Tarzan could tell the continuous rumble from the mountain was a little louder. Perhaps it was angered by the chaos he had caused deep below?

Carrying the woman over his shoulder, he trudged on through the jungle, back toward the Mangani. The mountain's business with Goyad and the apes was not his, and he didn't care how much the earth grumbled. He was lord of the jungle. He had nothing to fear.

. . .

R obbie had been more than irritated when Clark suggested he and Jane leave so the adults could discuss business terms with Lord Greystoke. It was clear he thought they would try to sabotage negotiations, and the others were still unaware that Jane had been awake during the entire conversation.

The smarmy Edward had appeared and guided them across the mining site to another set of cabins. Floodlights lit the site, attracting swarms of insects, but allowing the workers to maximize their workday. Edward kept to a wooden walkway that spanned the mud. Streams of dirty water ran beneath them. Off to one side, a group of Mbuti pygmies stood up to their chests in the dirty water, hauling large dishes from the brown murk as if panning for gold.

"What are they doing?" Jane asked Edward. Robbie recognized her tone; it was enthusiastic interest with a hint of flirting—exactly what she employed when she wanted her own way.

Edward had obviously forgotten how curt she had been before and returned her smile. *Sucker,* Robbie thought.

"They're washing the mud away so they can reach the heavier coltan beneath."

"So they don't actually mine it?"

"Not in the way you think. Coltan is found close to the surface. Here, all you have to do is sluice the mud away and you can retrieve it. The bulldozers help shift the surface mud off, but it's still a very labour-intensive process."

"I guess the pygmies make a lot from doing this?"

Edward shrugged. "We pay them one hundred and fifty dollars."

"A hundred-fifty bucks a day?" asked Robbie incredulously. He suddenly thought he was in the wrong line of work.

Edward laughed dismissively. "Per month." He caught Jane's horrified expression and added, "Most Congolese earn about ten dollars a month."

They reached the far end of the walkway and Edward took a detour that led to a large steel hopper brimming with unremarkable black stone, forming chips no bigger than gravel. Edward smiled and scooped the ore into his palm.

"Columbite-tantalite. Or coltan to you and me. It's currently selling at two hundred and thirty dollars a kilo. Sometimes the market can push it up as high as six hundred."

"You must be proud," said Jane, although Edward failed to detect her caustic tone.

Edward slowly poured the coltan from his palm. "Of course. We're out here helping technology push forward. Without this, civilization as we know it would be unable to function. We'd be back to Victorian engineering—no computers, no TV, nothing." He carefully wiped his hand, making certain every last grain fell back into the hopper, then nodded toward a close-by cabin. "Lord Greystoke wanted you to make yourselves comfortable in here."

The cabin was large and empty, lined with picnic-style benches to form a utilitarian canteen for the staff. The shutters to the kitchen were down and several dirty windows cast mottled light into the room, adding to the depressed atmosphere.

Edward hung at the door as Robbie and Jane entered. "I'll be back soon. I'm sure Lord Greystoke will conclude his business swiftly." He closed the door.

Jane let out a long sigh as she leaned against a table. "This is crazy! What are we going to do?"

"Why should we do anything? If Clark wants to lead them toward a volcano, good for him. I vote we head back to camp, contact Tarzan, and tell him to keep his head down."

"You don't get it, do you?" said Jane, exasperated. "The volcano is where Tarzan took his family. That's where the new feeding grounds are, and now we're gonna lead Sir Stuck-up right to them!"

Robbie peered through the window. He couldn't see much due to the thick grime coating it, just Edward's receding back as he crossed the walkway.

"Greystoke said he wasn't really interested in Tarzan," said Robbie thoughtfully. "I don't trust that Edward guy," he added as he lost sight of the man.

"He's a slimeball, just like Greystoke. And I don't believe a word

Greystoke said either. His dad was desperate to find Tarzan. He paid Rokoff to hunt him down—so why wouldn't he be as ruthless?"

"I don't know," muttered Robbie distractedly. He was still peering through the window. Something didn't feel right, but he couldn't put his finger on it.

Jane continued. "Look at what they've done to this place. Do you think if they find this city they'd be interested in its archeological value? Oh sure, that Werper probably is—but he's in for a shock when it gets bulldozed down for coltan."

"Greystoke was keen to get rid of us."

"Of course. He knows we won't agree to help him and that we'll try to put Clark and Dad off."

Something nagged at the back of Robbie's mind, an idea to which he couldn't quite latch on. A look Greystoke gave him, an offhand comment that sounded wrong. "He probably thinks we'd sabotage the expedition."

"Exactly," said Jane.

Then it hit Robbie, the idea that had been bothering him. "Exactly. Why would he want us around?" His mind was racing. He suddenly remembered Greystoke had used Clark's legal name, a name he'd long since dropped. Greystoke had done his research. On all of them.

Jane looked puzzled. "You think he's going to try and send us back to the camp?"

Robbie caught sight of movement through the window. Edward was returning with another man. He tried to wipe the glass for a clearer view, but the dirt was on the outside. "He knows that wouldn't work. He knows we'd warn Tarzan."

Jane shrugged. "So what can he do? Hold us hostage?" Even as she said the words the reality of the statement sank in.

"Worse," muttered Robbie as the door to the canteen opened and Edward walked back inside with a man in his fifties. The man's red sunburn indicated he hadn't had time to acclimate to the tropics.

"Mr. Canler?" said the man with a grin that revealed a missing tooth. He spoke in a soft Midwestern accent. "You led me on a merry chase—up rivers, around Uganda. . . . But here we are."

"Who are you?" asked Jane.

The man's eyes never left Robbie, and the smile never left his face. "You can call me Baxter. Private detective, although I prefer the term 'bounty hunter.' Has a cooler ring to it, don't you think? I have an arrest warrant for you, Mr. Canler. You're wanted for murder in New York. And I'm here to bring you back home."

9

By daybreak, Tarzan grew concerned for the female. She still had not awoken and her skin burned with a fever. He placed her in the shade offered by a small cave, and the Mangani sniffed at her, but otherwise gave her a wide berth. Except little Karnath, who warily approached. His trust in strangers had been stretched to breaking point after Nikolas Rokoff had abducted him, but still, the little ape mustered his courage and edged closer, gingerly poking the woman with a stick to elicit a response.

Tarzan kept one eye on the woman, the other on the dense jungle. He was anticipating a merciless Targarni reprisal, but none came. He pondered the strange woman who seemed to lead the Targarni. Who was she? Was she like him—raised in the wild? Or was she an outsider like Jane, who had come to love the jungle as much as he did? The thought of Goyad putting up with interference from a human confused Tarzan. There must be more to the underground city than he could fathom.

It was clear the female's condition was growing worse, despite the herbs that Tarzan had gathered that should ease such a fever. He started to feel a sense of responsibility; after all, he had saved her from death, so to have her die while in his care didn't seem right. Perhaps this was something Jane could help with. Tarzan might not know all the technology the loggers had, but he had seen enough to know there were some things beyond even his understanding. Besides, it had been too long since he had last seen Jane.

Tarzan was confident that a Targarni attack was not forthcoming. He left the unconscious female with the apes and sprinted for the trees. With one mighty leap he vaulted into the low-slung branches. The momentum spun him around higher and deeper into the jungle canopy.

. . .

It was dawn, and events moved at a rapid pace. Baxter roughly grabbed Robbie and shoved him against the wall.

"Get off me!" growled Robbie. But before he could strike out, he felt steel snap around his wrists as Baxter deftly handcuffed him.

Jane tried to pull Baxter off, but the man was stronger than he looked and held her back, though not before she had delivered a stinging slap across his cheek.

"The warrant's for him only, but I dare say the judge would be interested in whoever was aiding him," he snarled, rubbing his cheek.

Jane tensed, ready to strike again, but Robbie shook his head. "Don't, Jane. This isn't your fight."

"Good boy," said the private detective mockingly. "Just remember, being one step ahead don't make you any smarter than me, boy." He dangled the handcuff keys tantalizingly in front of Robbie, and then slipped them into his pocket. He turned to Jane. "Any last words?"

"You're making a mistake," Jane muttered, not taking her eyes off him.

Baxter hesitated. There was a hint of wild rage behind the girl's blue eyes. Something feral that unsettled him. He quickly composed himself and led Robbie to a secure room without another word.

• • •

Jane sat sullenly as Greystoke told Archie and Clark that Robbie was wanted in connection to the death of his sister and attempted murder of his stepfather. Archie was shocked and Clark admitted to having suspicions about the boy since he'd found him stowed away on the freighter that had brought the loggers to Africa. He'd never spoken up, believing that most people deserved a second chance.

Jane tried to tell them the truth. Robbie's younger sister, Sophie, had died of neglect under the hands of his drunken mother and abusive stepfather. Robbie had found her dead and attacked his stepfather, then fled America. Robbie had thought he'd accidentally killed his stepfather, but the burden of murder had been lifted from his shoulders when he discovered the man was still alive. However, his stepfather had twisted the facts and accused Robbie of murdering Sophie and attempting to murder him, neatly shifting the blame from himself and getting revenge in one fell swoop.

Archie and Clark found Jane's explanation dubious, although Clark was willing to give Robbie the benefit of the doubt and wanted to talk to him.

"I'm afraid that is not possible," said Greystoke flatly.

"I don't see why not," said Archie, keen to ease tensions now that a deal with Greystoke had been agreed upon.

"Because Mr. Canler is a liability," said Greystoke. "I have given Baxter full authority to keep him here until I return. Then we will ship him to the United States—"

"You'll just keep him prisoner here?" Jane was aghast.

Greystoke waved his hand dismissively and continued. "Where he will face legal proceedings. And much better here than locked in some Congolese jail, don't you think?" He placed a hand on Jane's shoulder and smiled warmly. "Whatever you may think of me, I am no monster. He'll be treated well."

Jane shucked him off. "It's rather strange that Baxter tracked him down here, isn't it? Here at your mine. Quite a coincidence."

Greystoke's smile vanished so suddenly Jane wondered if she had imagined it. "I placed my life in the hands of that *accused* murderer, and he deliberately led us astray. I think your father would be relieved not to have his only daughter mix with such company." He smiled as he turned to Archie. "Perhaps you should return to your camp and explain what has happened. They will be worried."

Clark wagged his finger. "Now wait a second, pal. You ain't shipping us off just so we have to rely on your good word that you didn't find anythin' at Opar. Besides, it ain't like I'll be drawin' you a map, is it?"

"Very well, you come along and lead the way." His eyes darted to Clark's injured leg. "I only hope you don't slow us down." He turned to Archie. "And perhaps you could stay here with your daughter and await our return?"

Archie considered for a moment before nodding in agreement. Jane wanted to insist on going with them—but she couldn't leave Robbie to his fate. Already she was trying to concoct a plan to spring him from Greystoke's prison. It was times like this when she really needed Tarzan to show up. She hoped he wouldn't let her down now.

An hour later, Greystoke's safari was under way. Werper and Idra had spent most of the night putting together the equipment. It was more than they could carry alone, so six Mbuti pygmies had been enlisted as porters. Idra was apparently some kind of expedition expert and had packed food, a satellite phone, a pair of rafts, which could be inflated into rigid-hulled powerboats to navigate the endless jungle rivers, and several waterproof boxes filled with Werper's scientific gear.

Clark had asked why the helicopter or floatplane couldn't be used to take them the whole way; it would have been easier to identify the volcano from the air. Greystoke had explained that they were traveling beyond the chopper's range; plus, there was no likelihood of finding a clear patch of ground to which they could be airdropped even half the way. The plane had a longer range, but again there was no guarantee they could find a stretch of water safe enough to land on. Worst-case, the machines were on standby should they need to be airlifted out in a hurry—at least if they were on the ground they could clear a landing area or judge if a body of water had any unwelcome surprises just below the surface.

Archie put his arm around Jane's shoulder as Clark, Greystoke, Werper, Idra, and the six porters crossed the muddy mining site and disappeared into the jungle.

"I'm kinda glad we're not hacking our way through there," said Archie with forced levity. "I've done enough jungle to last me a life-time."

Jane didn't say anything. She was hatching a plan to follow the group once she had freed Robbie.

. . .

Although Archie acted relaxed, Jane knew he was keeping a sharp eye on her. Edward hovered around, now flanked by two large Congolese security guards with unsmiling faces. Another was permanently positioned outside the cabin Robbie was housed in. Jane saw Baxter twice, no doubt eager not to stray too far from his payday. Freeing Robbie was going to be tougher than she had anticipated. The easiest approach was to wait until nightfall then sneak her way past the guard, but for every minute she wasted, Greystoke was a step closer to the Savage Lands, Tarzan, and poten-tially destroying the apes' home.

Several times, Jane thought she caught movement in the trees and her heart jumped with excitement, convinced it was Tarzan. But if the ape-man didn't show himself, it was for reasons she couldn't understand. The movement was becoming so frequent that she realized she'd probably been watching monkeys at play in the trees. The thought that Tarzan wasn't about to save the day made her more resolved than ever. It was up to her.

Toward lunchtime, the Mbuti workers stopped and took shelter in the canteen from the beating sun. Archie tried to cajole Jane into eating, but she refused. He knew better than to argue with her, so sat with Edward to eat. Baxter joined them, and soon the three men were talking animatedly.

This was her chance. The lone security guard sat outside the cabin, everybody else was distracted by their hungry bellies. She had to act now, but was still stuck for a plan. She had found a pair of bolt cutters she hoped could slice through Robbie's handcuffs, but they were useless against the security goon, who was almost twice her size. There was no way she could beat him in a fight. She looked around, desperate for something—anything—to reveal itself. Then she saw it, her weapon of choice.

Double-checking the coast was clear, Jane darted across the muddy site, almost losing her balance. She hid behind a bulldozer. Peering over the dirty yellow monstrosity to check that she hadn't been seen, she gripped the external handrails and hauled herself into the cab. Her foot slipped on the wide mud-slick caterpillar tracks, and—for one precarious moment—she was hanging from the cab, legs flailing. She regained her foothold and hoisted herself into the driver's seat. It bounced under her weight, a series of springs and tension cables designed to give the driver a smooth ride no matter what the terrain.

She had sat in the cab of the bulldozer at Karibu Mji many times, although she had been forbidden to drive it. It had been a rare place of solitude. Her hand found the seat adjustment control, which had been set up for the short stature of the Mbuti who had been driving. The key was in the ignition and she had watched Mr. David and the loggers drive their dozer so many times that she had a rough idea of what to do.

When Jane turned the key, the machine shuddered to life, black smoke spewing from the stack at the back of the cab as she revved the engine. She glanced through the grubby windshield and saw everybody was still inside eating, and not paying the slightest bit of attention to her. The sound of machinery at the mine was so common that nobody would question it.

She found the throttle lever on the right and slid it forward, the engine responding with a satisfying roar. This machine was much more advanced than the one back at camp, but the basic principles looked the same. Jane gripped the control lever and pushed forward—the machine moved without question. It gently rocked over the uneven terrain, but it felt more comfortable than most cars she had been in. The blade at the front of the dozer grazed the ground, which would only slow her down, so Jane pulled the right-hand joystick back to raise it and felt the machine spur on a little faster.

Still, nobody paid any attention to the bulldozer speeding toward them. Jane jogged the controls to the left, changing direction toward the cabin Robbie was in. Her thumb found the gear selector switch on the joystick and she moved up a gear, the dozer gaining pace. It was all automatic, so there was no messing with a clutch. In fact it was almost too late when she remembered the only pedal she needed was the decelerator, which served more as a brake.

She jogged the joystick to the left some more, lining up both the canteen and cabin in her sights. The guard looked up twice before thinking anything was amiss. Jane raised the bulldozer blade farther up and punched the horn when she was just yards away.

Now everybody turned to see the bulldozer veering toward them. She was relieved to see Archie move first, pulling Baxter to his feet as the bulldozer's blade slammed into the side and roof of the canteen. She didn't want to hurt anyone, just create a diversion. She could only imagine her father's complaints if he was hurt.

Inside, Jane barely felt a jolt as the dozer tore through the canteen's supporting wall—half outside, half inside. Workers fled as the caterpillar track flattened the tables they had been eating at. Wood groaned and the roof suddenly collapsed at an angle since there was one less wall to support it. Jane had noticed it was made from thin panels, designed to do nothing more than keep the rain out, so as it collapsed on the fleeing workers within, she hoped they wouldn't suffer anything more severe than a few bruises. But, if Tarzan had taught her anything, it was that only the wiliest survived.

Just fifteen feet ahead was the cabin with Robbie inside. She saw the guard pull a sidearm pistol—obviously following strict orders—and fire at her. She ducked, hitting the horn again and praying the stubborn guard would move aside in time.

The first bullet pinged off the blade; the second shattered the toughened windshield, spraying her with safety glass. Still crouched low, she couldn't see where she was going, but through the open side door she saw the guard leap into the mud to avoid being crushed. She reached for the horn again, but missed as the cab jolted when it struck the cabin. She only hoped Robbie had heard her coming.

The blade tore a chunk from the side of the cabin and the structure collapsed against the vehicle. Jane killed the engine, preventing the cabin from falling any further. Robbie had jumped into the far corner of what proved to be a supply room. He looked at her with wide eyes and for a moment Jane thought he was about to run from her. Then he burst into laughter.

"We're gonna be in so much trouble!" he quipped as he clambered over fallen crates, stepping up into the cab. The handcuffs hampered him and when he reached Jane, she pulled the bolt cutters from the floor. Jamming the chain between the blades, she squeezed the cutter's arms together and the chain broke after a brief resistance. Robbie still had the two cuffs on his wrists, but at least he was free to move.

"Come on!" said Jane breathlessly, still not quite believing her plan had worked. "We're going to have to run."

They leaped from the cab, splashing into the mud, and sprinted for the trees. It was a slog, their feet bogging down with each step. Behind, the workforce was still escaping from the collapsed canteen. The crowd was jostling Archie and only the three burly guards had enough presence of mind to race toward the fleeing figures.

"Come on!" encouraged Jane, as Robbie almost tumbled in the mud. The trees were just ahead.

Then from behind, Baxter's voice carried across the site. "Shoot them! Don't let them get away!"

Jane risked a glance behind as two of the guards drew their pistols. The one Jane had almost flattened ran toward them with an expression of hatred. Shots suddenly rang out as one of the guards opened fire—but he was too wide, intent on not shooting his comrade.

"In the leg, you moron!" Baxter screamed. "Don't kill them!"

Jane ducked as she ran. Another glance behind and she saw her father launch from the canteen wreckage and tackle the shooter into the mud.

"NO!" yelled Archie as he fell hard onto the goon.

Baxter was just behind him, focused on Robbie. But he tripped over the fallen men and landed flat on his face in the mud and found himself entangled with the raging Archie.

"WHOA!" Robbie yelled, suddenly slipping in the mud. He tried to scramble to his feet, but lost precious seconds slip-sliding. Jane doubled back to pull him upright.

The towering angry goon was almost upon them. He glared at Jane with so much hatred she was convinced he wanted to tear her apart with his bare hands. She hauled Robbie up, but they had nowhere to go. Their escape plan had been foiled.

The Congolese man reached for her neck with a massive hand. Then his eyes suddenly bulged, anger turning to pain as he reeled backward with an arrow in his shoulder. A further volley of arrows flew overhead, forcing the remaining guard to change direction and run to the bulldozer for cover. Archie and the gun-toting guard quickly gave up their struggle and crawled toward the safety of the wrecked canteen to avoid the rain of arrows that peppered the ground. Baxter cowered, his arms over his head as he whimpered. The arrows landed around them, but none hit. Not due to bad marksmanship, but intention.

Jane and Robbie spun around to see a pygmy warrior, dressed in plain, traditional loincloth and with bow in hand, wave them nearer. It was the same warrior who had stalked them through the jungle and stolen their provisions. How he had found them again was anybody's guess, but right now, the pygmies looked like a more pleasant option than the mining camp.

Jane hauled Robbie fully to his feet and they raced into the jungle, circled as they ran by a dozen armed pygmies.

10

Keeping pace with the pygmies was tough work and sweat was soon pouring from Jane and Robbie as they crashed through the foliage. The pygmies' diminutive size was an asset in the jungle; they seldom had to duck under the low boughs and they never made a sound as they passed. Their camouflage was so perfect that Jane couldn't tell how many of the warriors escorted them; they were mere flickers of movement in the foliage, just enough to guide them onward.

The pygmies must have sensed their wards were tiring because the leader stopped in a clearing with a silver stream running through it, cascading down from a small waterfall. Robbie thrust his head in the water to cool off and drink heavily. Jane splashed the water across her face and took a moment to catch her breath. Then she looked at the pygmy leader. He stood several yards away, watching her with a curious expression.

"I know you don't understand me," she said. "But thank you for helping us." She hoped their intentions were good as she couldn't quite shake Greystoke's tales of cannibalistic tribes deep in the jungle.

The pygmy cocked his head back, his eyes always on Jane, and spoke to somebody in the trees. Jane heard the reply, but could see nobody. Then the leader stepped forward and pulled some strips of dried meat from a pouch at his waist. He offered them to Jane.

"Eat." The word sounded clumsy in his mouth.

Jane took the strips, and handed one to Robbie. He sniffed at it suspiciously, but Jane tore a strip off and chewed, not wanting to offend their new friends.

"You speak English?"

The pygmy smiled and nodded, clearly pleased with his linguistic skills. "Some. It is wise to learn the language of your enemy."

Jane glanced at Robbie, determined to show no fear, as Werper's stories played out in her imagination. "We're not your enemies."

"No. Greystoke is the enemy. He threw my people from our own lands and will not let us return."

"Then Greystoke is our mutual enemy," said Robbie who had risked nibbling a corner of the dried meat and was satisfied with the taste. He extended his hand. "My name's Robbie. This is Jane," he said nodding to Jane.

"I am Orando," the pygmy said. He fixed his gaze back on Jane. "And you are a forest goddess?"

Robbie spluttered with laugher and shook Jane's shoulder. "Her? Ha! I never heard that one before." He jerked his thumb at Orando and continued laughing as he spoke to Jane. "This little guy thinks you're awesome."

Jane felt her cheeks flush and she couldn't match Orando's intense gaze. "I don't know about that," she mumbled.

Orando pointed a pair of fingers at his own eyes. "I have seen. You tamed Numa. Only a god has such power."

Now Jane understood. "Oh, Numa . . . No, I've encountered him before. . . ." She trailed off, suddenly realizing he had used Tarzan's word. "Where did you hear the name 'Numa' before?"

"That's the Lion God's name," he said simply.

"I've only heard Tarzan use that name before. Do you know him?"

Orando didn't seem surprised that Jane had mentioned Tarzan. "Tarzan is *Munango-Keewati*, the Jungle God."

Hundreds of questions now buzzed around Jane's head. Tarzan had said he'd only ever encountered a few people before. Had the pygmies helped raise him? That would account for a number of the ape-man's impressive survival skills. But the most pressing question made it to her lips.

"Where is Tarzan? We have to find him. He's in great danger."

• • •

Clark had given vague directions the expedition could follow as they set out. He trailed at the back of the party, his progress still hampered by his injured leg, but he refused to mention the pain shooting through it, instead relying on the wooden stick Mr. David had carved for him. Greystoke kept close, recognizing Clark's difficulty and lending him a hand whenever he could. Clark couldn't decide if it was a genuine act of kindness, or just that Greystoke didn't want anything to happen to him before they found Opar. Idra was always at the back, a hunting rifle over her shoulder. Conversation was kept to a minimum as they focused on the steps ahead.

They took short but frequent breaks. The Mbuti sat away, always somber, never complaining, never exhausted. Greystoke sat beside Clark and offered his water bottle. He followed Clark's gaze to Idra who was stalking around the perimeter of their pit stop, eyeing the trees for danger.

"Don't you ever put your feet up?" Clark quipped. But Idra stared at him blankly.

"She's like that with everyone," Greystoke confided. "Heck of a shot, though. Should we need her." Clark didn't reply and Greystoke didn't appear to enjoy the silence. "I'm sorry about your boy Robert."

Clark was thoughtful for a moment before speaking up. "Jane was right. Quite a coincidence, Baxter turning up with you."

"My family's business interests here are legitimate. Or as legitimate as anything can be as this country tears itself apart with internal feuding. It serves to stay on the right side of people, and Baxter had been applying a certain amount of pressure on the authorities here. I could hardly deny helping a US law enforcer, could I? You believe Robbie is innocent?"

"Yeah. After everythin' we've been through out 'ere, I think Robbie's shown his real colors. Even if it meant goin' behind my back." Clark was still angry that Robbie had interfered with their plans to cash in on the Greystoke estate, but on the other hand, he admired his spirit. It reminded Clark of how he used to act: a young free agent at large in the world. Everything had been at his feet, and an adventure was waiting around every corner. He'd always been chasing fortune and glory; even now, being out in the wilderness searching for a lost city was something he used to dream of doing. But age and his injury were wearing him down. He had hoped that finding Tarzan would be an easy venture, and he prayed that this would be his last hike through the jungle.

"So what will you do with this lost city?" he asked, aiming his question at Werper.

The Belgian broke from his reverie and took a swig from his water bottle before answering. "It's my life's quest. Others mocked the idea of a jungle civilization thriving out here." He indicated to the deep forest. "Here, of all places, the cradle of civilization, where man first stepped down from the trees. Opar will earn me my rightful place amongst scientific circles. Howard Carter and Albert Werper will be the names they teach in history classes."

"So you ain't interested in the treasure," Clark asked calculatingly.

Werper hesitated, just enough for Clark to read the unspoken greed underneath Werper's ambitions. "Some money would be an advantage. But money doesn't buy your legacy in the history books, does it?" The last was aimed firmly at Greystoke.

Clark studied Greystoke. For a split second, the loathing he felt for Werper was written all over his face. Greystoke quickly recovered his composure.

"You must forgive Albert. He does not believe in my family's right to our title." His gaze never left Werper, as if daring him to speak. "He believes wealth and power should not be handed down through families." He turned to Werper, treating him to a thin smile.

"You forget, Albert, I have always been fascinated with the legend of Opar and am fully financing *your* passion to be here." Werper's jaw clenched, but he didn't retaliate. Instead he stared at the floor.

Clark turned back to Greystoke. "And Tarzan? How does he fit into the picture? I mean, Opar changes everything, right?"

Werper's head snapped up and a nasty smile crossed his face. "Ah, yes. The *rightful* Lord Greystoke. How does he fit into your plans?"

William Greystoke scowled at Werper. But before he could comment, Idra walked across holding a satellite phone.

"I called our position into camp and they have a problem."

"Need I be there to solve everything for them?"

"The Canler boy escaped from custody. It appears the girl drove a bulldozer through half the cabins to spring him." There was a hint of admiration in her voice.

Greystoke quickly stood. "What?"

"Edward thinks they're heading this way."

Even Werper's cynical smile vanished. "If they get to Opar before us, it could prove problematic."

Clark stood up, confused as to why everybody was so concerned. "Why is that a problem? We simply won't get there in the first place."

Greystoke was furious. "Those two have done nothing but throw a wrench in the works. Having them roam free will not help us at all." He snatched the satellite phone from Idra and punched in a number. "Get ready to move out. The rest break is over."

• • •

The pygmies' knowledge of the land was invaluable and Robbie and Jane's progress was swift. Orando stayed with them, but the other pygmies remained unseen, dashing ahead into the jungle to clear the path. They made rapid progress along a network of animal trails, only stopping once when they caught up with a scout who was kneeling, examining broken branches. They talked rapidly, the scout pointing to indentations in the mud. Orando translated.

"People have moved through here very recently." He indicated to a branch that had been cleanly severed through as somebody had pushed by. "Ten people. One who walks with a stick . . ."

"Clark," said Robbie.

"This is Greystoke's party," Jane added. "How far ahead are they?"

Orando rubbed the leaking sap from the branch between his fingers, judging how long ago it had been cut. "Not too far. They move slowly, like clumsy elephants. We will overtake today."

Jane started down the track, following the wake of Greystoke's safari. "Then we can't waste any time. Let's go."

Orando pointed off at a forty-five-degree angle. "This way. Their trail takes them through the swamp. Faster this way."

Without another word, he began to follow a faint track through the bush that had been invisible to Jane.

• • •

Midges circled Clark's head with a monotonous buzz. He swatted at them and slapped his neck, killing another blood-hungry pest, but his cheek and the right side of his neck were already covered in itchy bite marks after five minutes of being in the swamp.

After a several hours' march, the trees petered out into a wide area of marshland. Greystoke told them it was part of the river where they had been airlifted from the day before, but they were farther upstream in a tributary. Once through the marsh, he promised they would have some relief, as he had called in the floatplane to meet them at the river. They would have to find a clear stretch of water for it to land on, but Greystoke was gambling that, if it could take them even just five miles farther, they would have enough of a lead over Robbie and Jane.

As Clark waded through the foul water that came above his knees and stank like dirty laundry, he was beginning to think Robbie and Jane would have no trouble overtaking them. The others were struggling too, but none more than the Mbuti porters who were up to their midriffs and constantly getting bogged down with the heavy equipment.

"We should break the boats out," said Werper as he stumbled through the mire, briefly sinking his arm into the water and lifting it out with three leeches the size of his fingers clinging to his arm. He swore in French and yanked one off, only succeeding in ripping the soft body in half, leaving the head anchored to his skin.

"Leave it," Clark cautioned. "You'll only get another bite, an' you don't wanna infect the wound with this dirty water."

Greystoke ignored Werper's discomfort; he was focused only on his own. "We can't break the boats out yet. We need solid ground to inflate them, and the engines will just get choked up in this stuff."

They pressed on, everybody muttering in a variety of languages as they stumbled through. Several times, Clark saw movement in the water, the still surface rippling menacingly. He feared a crocodile attack, but nothing happened.

After hours of toil, the water became shallower and they saw solid ground ahead, bathed in the red hues of the lowering sun. They all clambered out and dropped to the ground, exhausted, removing the leeches still clinging to them. A pair of cigarette lighters were passed around the group and used to burn the leeches' heads so their jaws unlocked and they fell off with ease. Idra broke out a large first-aid kit filled with field dressings, antivenom, and a range of medicine to keep an army afloat. She disinfected her wounds, then tended to Greystoke and Clark. She clearly had no fondness for Werper or the Mbuti because she handed the antiseptic and gauze to them so they could tend to their own problems.

Only when they had cleaned up and were ready to press on did Clark glance back at the swamp and notice a huge crocodile basking in the dying light. It was the largest specimen he had ever seen, the armor-plated skin and mouthful of jagged teeth hinting at its prehistoric heritage. It was a lethal predator and they had been fortunate it hadn't been hunting them.

They headed upstream, keen to get away from the midges and stench of the swamp, before finally settling down on the bank and lighting a fire so they could eat and dry out. Greystoke radioed the floatplane and everybody settled back, exhausted and in pain.

• • •

Clark had nodded off, only waking when the sound of the plane buzzed into his consciousness. Idra had identified a length of water she judged to be deep enough and she guided the aircraft in with glowing batons so the pilot could judge the touchdown.

The aircraft banked low and lined itself up to the straight section of river, startling a flock of long-necked wading birds on the riverbank. With minimal fuss, the pilot landed, the two pontoons skimming along the surface as the plane came to a graceful stop. The pilot idled the twin engines, steering the aircraft toward the bank. In the late afternoon, the two propellers sounded like buzz saws and Clark could hear the blood pulsing in his ears the moment they stopped.

Greystoke took the rope offered by the copilot and, with the porters' help, they dragged the aircraft closer to the bank and secured it on a log that had washed ashore.

Clark watched as the discussion between the pilots and Lord Greystoke grew heated.

"They don't wanna fly tonight," he guessed, sharing his thoughts with Werper. But the Belgian wasn't listening. He was looking around for Idra, who had vanished into the jungle with a box of equipment. Greystoke stalked back to the others, gesturing helplessly.

"They say we can't fly until dawn!"

Clark didn't blame them. "If you don't know if there's any suitable landing place, then it would be suicide." He could see Greystoke accepted the logic, but could tell he just didn't like it. "I, for one, feel safer with my feet on the ground at night."

"If they get ahead . . ."

Clark held up his hand to try to calm Greystoke. "If they get ahead, so what? We can hop farther across the jungle in this, and it won't have to be much farther to stay ahead. Besides, I can't see them crossing this river at night, can you?"

Greystoke sighed then ordered the porters to set the tents up. They would be spending the night on the riverbank after all.

. . .

Jane didn't find the darkness of the jungle frightening. The constant hum of the insects and frogs that populated the night felt like a comforting blanket. They had stopped to make camp as the sun dipped behind the trees, casting deep shadows across the jungle.

Six pygmy scouts joined Orando at the fire, and Jane wondered how many remained unseen. They had hunted a small buck that they roasted over the fire, and soon everybody had eaten their fill and relaxed, warmed by the flames. During the hike, Jane had thought of yet more questions regarding the pygmies and Tarzan.

"How long have you known Tarzan?" she asked. The question had distracted her for most of the journey.

Orando smiled enigmatically. "*Munango-Keewati* fell from the sky and was raised by the Mangani. Our paths crossed when he was young. He has always been a friend of my people."

Jane pictured the airplane crashing into the jungle and tried to imagine what it must have been like for the pygmies, who had never encountered civilization.

Robbie poked the fire with a stick, watching a flurry of embers dance into the night sky. He attempted the word, "*Munango-cutie* . . ."

"*Keewati*," Orando corrected with a smile.

"*Keewati*," repeated Robbie carefully. "The Jungle God. You mean like a spirit?"

"There are spirits and gods all around us," said Orando simply. "Some we see, some we fear, and some guide us."

"But that name," persisted Robbie. "Is that a pygmy name?"

The question confused Orando. "It has always been handed from shaman to shaman, father to son. A name discovered by our ancestors."

Robbie looked calculating. "Would they be from Opar?" Jane

didn't like Robbie's line of questioning. She wondered just how much the stories of lost treasure were playing on his mind, but knew the subject had to come up at some point. "From the Savage Lands?"

Orando looked grim. "The Savage Lands are a place no man is meant to walk."

"But that's where we're headed," said Jane.

"Yes!" Orando nodded, then he smiled and looked at Jane. "But you are no man."

Robbie laughed, absently batting away a mosquito. "That's right, you're a goddess."

"Tell me something I don't know," Jane whispered back playfully.

Orando caught the light glimmering from the cuffs on Robbie's wrists. He leaned forward and examined them.

"You like them?" Robbie asked. "You can have them if you can get them off."

"You are no god," said Orando. "Just a man." Robbie shrugged amiably; it was a statement rather than an insult. "But you walk with gods."

"That's how I like to roll," said Robbie with a smile.

Suddenly, a scout sprinted into clearing and spoke urgently. Orando intently listened to the scout. Then he turned to Jane. "They have found Greystoke's camp an hour from here." He pointed into the darkness. "If we leave now, we can overtake them."

11

Clark found it almost impossible to sleep in the tent. The humidity had risen to unbearable levels and, when he flicked his camp lantern on, he saw the silhouette of hundreds of bugs clinging to his mosquito net.

He lay on his back and stared at the curved roof, wishing he could get some rest before the arduous trek tomorrow. After what seemed like an hour, his eyes began to flutter as he felt the welcoming wave of slumber smother him. He was just on the edge of consciousness when a piercing scream suddenly rang across the jungle. It was so high and constant he jolted upright, immediately awake. Through the fabric of the tent he could see a bright light burning. Then he heard raised voices—Greystoke and Werper shouting. He scrambled for the tent zip and, with some difficulty, clambered out.

Powerful floodlights illuminated the trees and what Clark had thought was a scream was an electronic alarm. Its warble abruptly cut off. Greystoke and Werper stared into the trees, while the Mbuti porters kept a safe distance away, unsure what was happening. The pilots hung close to the floatplane in which they were sleeping; the copilot had a pistol drawn.

"What's goin' on?" said Clark in a hushed voice as he drew level to Greystoke.

Greystoke kept his gaze on the trees as he spoke. "Something tripped Idra's security."

That answered Clark's question about what was in the case she had hauled into the jungle. Remembering Greystoke's reaction to the pygmies, Clark assumed he was probably frightened for his own life more than the lives of his expedition members.

Clark saw movement. He had to shield his eyes against the floodlights, which had now attracted a tornado of insects. Figures emerged from the light, but he couldn't make out any detail until they had cleared the trees—and he was shocked to see Jane and Robbie with their hands on their heads. Idra walked behind, prompting them forward with the barrel of her hunting rifle.

"Look what I caught snooping around," she said.

Clark was alarmed, but refrained from making any comment. He was thankful Archie had been sent back to the logging camp. Too much was riding on his deal with Greystoke and he was relying on the Englishman for more than he cared to admit. At least Robbie and Jane didn't appear to be hurt.

Greystoke marched over, openly angry. "Do you know what damage you have caused?" He slapped Jane hard across the face, leaving a nasty red mark. Robbie moved to intercept, but was restrained as Idra jammed the barrel of her rifle into his ribs.

Clark clenched his fingers, ready to strike the man, but he held back. He could get his revenge on Greystoke after the Englishman paid up.

"You could have killed people with the stunt you pulled to free this . . . this criminal!" spittle flew from Greystoke's lips. Jane stared at him coolly. He raised his hand to strike her again.

Clark couldn't stand by and do nothing. "William . . . easy."

He saw Greystoke's hand tremble, but he lowered it as Clark's warning sank in. He turned to Robbie, treating him to a cold sneer.

"I shouldn't expect anything else from a reprobate like you." He looked between Jane and Robbie. "I'll have you both shipped back to where you belong." Then he looked quizzical. "You made it all the way here on your own?" He clearly didn't believe that. He turned to Idra and walked a few paces back, talking quietly. Idra's gun never moved from her captives. Clark wasn't sure she would shoot Robbie or Jane, but could tell from the look on Robbie's face that *he* believed she would.

Clark limped closer to them and delicately ran a finger down the red welt on Jane's cheek. She flinched but didn't make a sound.

"You really know how to get into trouble, don't ya? You definitely get that from your mum." That forced a small smile from Jane. Clark lowered his voice; he had known Jane all her life and, without Archie around, felt he had some vague parenting to do. "You OK?" she nodded. Clark motioned into the jungle. "What happened out there?"

"Oh the usual," said Jane with a sigh. "Destroyed a mining camp, escaped with a native tribe, explored the jungle . . ."

Robbie spoke up. "We had a few friends help us out. We activated the tripwires and the next thing I know they've melted into the jungle and she's pointing a gun at us," he said, nodding his head toward Idra.

Clark made sure he wasn't overheard as he spoke to Jane. "I don't expect you to understand." He turned to Robbie. "But *you*, I do. We got a lot ridin' on this, don't ya see? I don't like his lordship any more than you do, but I can put up with him until all this is over."

"You're all heart," said Jane sarcastically.

Clark's eyes narrowed in annoyance. "I'm not gonna see Robbie carted back to the States for some kangaroo court to judge him."

Robbie was surprised. "So you believe I'm innocent?"

Clark nodded. "I bet your stepdad had it comin' to 'im." He flicked a glance at Greystoke. "And I don't think he's got it in 'im to do anythin' about Tarzan. He just wants to see the title stays with 'im. All I ask is you both keep your heads down."

"That's enough, Clark," said Greystoke returning to them. "We'll tie them up for the night, then the pilots can take them back to camp in the morning."

"You're gonna tie us up . . . Out here?" asked Robbie incredulously. "Do you know what's in these woods?"

"Would you prefer to sleep in the airplane?" said Greystoke caustically. "Just be thankful Idra showed enough restraint not to blow your silly little heads off." Robbie glanced across to see Idra who winked mischievously at him then crouched down to a small device housed in a flight case tucked in a knot of plants; it was the tripwire control system.

Robbie lowered his hands. But a warning from the copilot now standing directly behind him, jabbing the barrel of a pistol into his ribs, made him change his mind.

"I don't have Idra's restraint," the copilot growled. He grabbed both of Robbie's wrists and pulled them behind Robbie's back.

"Over there," Lord Greystoke prompted, pointing toward a curved tree close to the water's edge.

"You won't get what you want from Opar," taunted Jane.

Greystoke's patience was wearing thin. "Perhaps I should gag you too? I think that may be an improvement for us all."

Jane goaded him. "You're real tough. Following in rich daddy's footsteps? He hired Rokoff to kill D'Arnot so he couldn't spread the word about Tarzan and let the world find out your family is a bunch of frauds." Greystoke tensed. "Afraid of losing your privileges? Because when I get out of here, I'm gonna make sure the world knows what kind of creep you really are."

With a fierce backhand, Greystoke struck her hard across the cheek again—just as Idra reset the perimeter defenses and the lights extinguished, leaving an orange afterglow in everybody's eyes.

Then, a mighty roar bellowed across the river. It was no wild beast, but it was barely human. It was a terrifying sound, so filled with rage and anguish that it chilled the blood of the entire group.

Clark rubbed his eyes, attempting to get his night vision back. But he could see nothing other than Robbie, Jane, and Greystoke directly in front of him.

For a moment, nothing stirred. Then came a whispering swish. Clark heard a gasp from the copilot who was restraining Robbie. The captor fell to the ground.

Greystoke fumbled for the flashlight attached to his belt. With shaking fingers he switched it on, the beam illuminating the copilot who was now writhing on the ground, an arrow through his shoulder and blood pooling into the dry mud. Greystoke whimpered with fright.

"The lights! Get the lights on!"

Idra was already lunging for the light controls. She activated them. The powerful floodlights shone directly in their faces, temporarily blinding them all. Some unseen hand had spun all the lights around. Blinded, Idra dropped the controls, which rolled into the grass around her feet.

Werper staggered, unseeing, and dropped to his knees. Clark covered his eyes with his arm to avoid being blinded. Greystoke grunted and reached out for Robbie and Jane as they both attempted to run. Robbie was out of his reach, but Greystoke's hand snagged Jane's shoulder and pulled her back. He slid his arm around her neck, tightly holding her like a human shield.

The Mbuti porters were shrieking in panic as something huge leaped into their midst. Clark saw one pygmy hurled aside like a ragdoll, quickly followed by a heavy packing case. Was a gorilla attacking them? The remaining five porters fled in different directions.

Idra swung her rifle from over her shoulder and shot toward their attacker. It was useless, so she turned the gun on the lights. Four perfect shots and the lights exploded in a shower of sparks.

Clark was still dazzled, but his vision slowly returned as darkness fell once again. He could just discern a menacing shadow stalking toward the group.

Still with one arm around Jane, Greystoke's free trembling hand found where the copilot's pistol had dropped. He raised it, pressing the barrel against Jane's neck.

"Don't come any closer!" His quivering voice betrayed his fear.

The figure paused—and was illuminated in a high-beam flashlight shone by the pilot.

It was Tarzan, standing just feet away. The ape-man's eyes burned with utter malice and a lion-like growl thundered from his barrel chest.

Seeing Tarzan and Greystoke together, Clark was shocked by the resemblance between the cousins. It was purely cosmetic—the same jaw, nose, piercing eyes. But where Tarzan's physique was the pinnacle of perfection, Lord Greystoke was a reed of a man—somebody who had lived in lavish comfort all his life.

"J—John?" Greystoke stammered. "My God, it really is you . . ." Tarzan took a step forward, causing Greystoke to shove the pistol so hard against Jane's neck that she whimpered. "St—stop. It doesn't have to be this way," he stammered.

Idra opened fire. A rifle shot blasted out, the bullet nicking Tarzan's arm. She had aimed wide, but wouldn't miss a second time.

There would be no second time.

Like a cat, Tarzan sprang away, out of the flashlight beam. The pilot had no hope of catching him with the light as he zigzagged toward Idra.

Greystoke didn't wait to see what would happen next. He dragged Jane toward the floatplane.

"Start the engines!" he yelled. "Start the damn engines!"

Clark hesitated to follow Greystoke as he watched Idra's fate. His night vision had returned just enough to see her fire another shot. Then Tarzan pounced, and the two figures rolled back into the night. He heard Tarzan bellow and Idra scream. But the sound was drowned out as the aircraft's twin propellers kicked into action.

Greystoke was bundling a struggling Jane aboard the aircraft before climbing in himself. Somebody had untied the anchor rope from the tree so the plane drifted out into the river as the engines revved. With the choice of escaping on the plane or being left to face the wrath of Tarzan, Clark quickly hobbled toward the craft, but his injured leg hampered his every step.

"Jane! No!" yelled Robbie as he sprinted toward the plane. He was much faster than Clark could have hoped to be. He splashed through the water, leaping onto the plane's pontoon as Greystoke tried to close the door.

"Get off!" Greystoke yelled, trying to boot Robbie into the water. Robbie sidestepped and pushed his body weight forward, butting Greystoke in the chest. They fell into the aircraft as the pilot angled away from the bank and spun the plane around, ready for take-off. The landing lights did little to illuminate the darkness ahead.

Clark splashed through the water, only venturing up to his knees. "WAIT!" he yelled, waving his arms. "COME BACK!"

Werper stood on the bank behind, waving a flashlight for attention. "WHERE'RE YOU GOING?" he demanded.

If the pilot or Greystoke could hear the protests, they made no response. The engines rose to full power and the aircraft began to move across the water. Clark suddenly became aware of movement behind him and spun around to see Tarzan illuminated in Werper's flashlight. The archeologist gave a strangled whimper as he stared death in the face. Clark limped to intervene.

"No, Tarzan! Mate, it's me, Clark!"

With a flicker of recognition, Tarzan hesitated. Then, without a word, he sprinted along the riverbank, on course for the aircraft.

12

From where Greystoke had thrown her on the floor, Jane jostled against the bare steel seat supports as the float-plane bounced across the water. The noise from the engines was almost deafening, but she could just make out the scuffle between Greystoke and Robbie.

She tried to sit up as the plane jounced over the water, but a severe jolt threw her back. She finally used a seat to pull herself up and saw Robbie and Greystoke wrestling in the confined space. Robbie repeatedly forced Greystoke's hand against the bulkhead until he released the pistol, which dropped and slid past Jane, disappearing toward the tail.

As she hauled herself farther up, intending to help Robbie, she caught a glimpse of trees through the side window. Darkness swallowed almost every detail, except the silhouettes of the trees against the moonlit clouds. They whipped past as the plane's speed increased. Jane also caught a fleeting glimpse of Tarzan running through the canopy and vaulting from bough to bough, but there was no way he could catch up—she had to slow the plane down somehow.

A thump from the cabin drew her attention back to Greystoke and Robbie locked together, arms crossed over each other's throats. Robbie punched a lion-claw wound, and Greystoke howled in pain, but didn't let go.

Jane capitalized on the movement of the plane keeping them both off balance. Gripping the seats on either side of the aisle, she catapulted herself into the struggling pair. All three fell into the cockpit. It was such a confined space that they shoved the pilot forward against the console, crushing him against the controls, forcing him to release the throttle control that hung down from the cabin ceiling.

The engines changed pitch and the aircraft pivoted to the left so quickly that one pontoon skipped off the river as the opposite wingtip ducked so low it sliced through the water. Now they were headed straight for the trees. The sudden shift in direction was enough to throw Robbie, Greystoke, and Jane off the pilot. He slowed the plane, steering it back out into the relative safety of the open river.

Greystoke now had Robbie pinned down, but wasn't strong enough to hold him in place and couldn't beat him in a fair fight. So he had to play dirty. The Englishman's free hand plucked a small fire extinguisher from the wall and struck Robbie across the head, knocking him unconscious. Greystoke glared at Jane. "Try anything like that again and I will throw you out when we're over the jungle." Turning to the pilot he snapped an order. "Get us in the air. Now!"

"I can't see where we're going. This is suicide!"

"Staying here would be sui—" A loud thump from the roof stopped him mid-sentence. The plane rocked as something landed on it.

The pilot eased back on the throttle. "I'll have to check that out."

Driven by fear, Greystoke lunged for the pilot's hand, shoving the roof-mounted throttle forward so fast the plane surged ahead.

"Trust me, you don't want to know what that was. Get us in the air now!"

All that could be seen through the windshield was the patch of river immediately ahead, illuminated by the aircraft's headlights. If there was anything farther in front, then there would be nothing they could do to avoid it.

Jane pressed herself against a side window to see if she could spot Tarzan. The aircraft's overhead wing meant she could see nothing except the spray of water from the pontoon caught in the landing light. Then, the rough ride suddenly stopped as they lifted from the water—just in time. A gnarled tree trunk sprouted from the river, but the pilot hadn't seen it. They all heard the squeal of metal as the starboard pontoon sheered off against the trunk.

Now they had no way to safely land. The pilot yanked back on the stick, pulling the aircraft up in a steep ascent the moment he realized they had reached a bend in the river. A solid wall of trees loomed ahead. The clatter of branches slashing the underside of the plane reverberated through the cabin—but suddenly stopped as they reached a safer altitude.

Greystoke had been forced back into a seat during the steep climb, his knuckles white as he held on to the seat in front. He let out the breath he had been holding as the aircraft banked around. Jane glimpsed moonlight on the river below, and then all was black as they leveled out.

The pilot shouted into the cabin. "The trees must have damaged the avionics. Nothing's working: wind speed, altitude . . ."

A colossal bang from the roof of the aircraft diverted everybody's attention.

"W—what in hell's name . . . ?" stammered the pilot. Suddenly, he jumped in his seat as Tarzan's face appeared over the edge of the cockpit, his eyes narrow slits against the wind, his hair rippled back from the acceleration of the plane.

"Shake him off!" ordered Greystoke.

The very idea went against the pilot's ethics. "No! He'll fall to his death!"

"It's him or us!" shouted Greystoke as he reached for the stick. The pilot snagged Greystoke's hand, but it was too late. The Englishman yanked the stick side to side, violently jerking the aircraft. Tarzan slipped from view.

"You'll kill us all!" the pilot protested. Before he could speak again, a fist slammed against the cockpit with jackhammer strength. Although the window was designed to withstand a crash, it was no match for Tarzan's might as he pile-drove it through. The pilot was strapped in with no chance of avoiding Tarzan's grasping hand. The ape-man grabbed the pilot's hair, driving his face into the controls so hard that several dials shattered. The unconscious pilot slumped against the console, forcing the plane into a sudden dive.

Jane screamed as her stomach lurched. She slid to the front of the cabin. Greystoke was already leaning into the cockpit, reaching around the prone pilot so he could level the aircraft out. He tried to climb into the copilot's seat, but Robbie's unconscious form was blocking the way. With some effort Greystoke pushed Robbie aside with one hand, keeping the other on the stick. Then he slid into the seat and, with slick palms, took control.

"Can you fly?" Jane asked, feeling more terrified than she had ever been.

"I've had a few lessons," said Greystoke, looking bewildered as he scanned the dials.

"How many?"

He hesitated for too long. "One," he finally admitted. "It was a birthday gift."

Jane felt oddly calm. She was sure they were going to die, but found herself able to focus on more immediate issues. Robbie lay on the floor, a bump on his head from where he had been struck. There was no sign of Tarzan.

"You've killed him," said Jane, suddenly horrified. "You've killed your own cousin."

"I didn't want to," Greystoke snapped defensively. "He was trying to kill me!"

Jane's next words froze on her lips as the aircraft's metal door suddenly buckled. Inside the cabin, it sounded like drums signifying approaching doom.

"What now?" whined Greystoke as he craned around to see what was happening.

A fist effortlessly smashed through the door's window. A muscular arm poked through and gripped the door, yanking it off its hinges. Tarzan swung inside, blood trickling from where Idra's bullet had glanced his arm, and glass from the cockpit windshield still embedded in his fist like brass knuckles.

With a single glance, Tarzan took in the cabin's situation and charged for Greystoke. One hand closed around Greystoke's neck, hauling him from the seat. His other hand was pulled back ready to deliver a blow that would knock the Englishman's head off.

"NO!" screamed Jane. Tarzan hesitated. Her voice was the only sound that could calm his rage. "Don't kill him," she said.

"He try to kill you," snarled Tarzan.

"It was a mistake," Jane assured him. She felt the plane gently lurch to port. Without anybody at the controls it was just a matter of time before they plunged into the jungle. Her eyes met Greystoke's, which were as wide as saucers. "Wasn't it?" she said, coaxing his answer. She was frightened for all their lives and, as much as she despised Greystoke, she had no desire to watch Tarzan kill him in cold blood—an act that would send the aircraft plummeting into the earth.

"Yes, yes," whimpered Lord Greystoke, his mouth dry. "A stupid accident . . . I'm your family, Tarzan. . . ."

Tarzan increased the pressure on Lord Greystoke's neck, choking the apology from him. Greystoke started to turn blue.

"Tarzan! No! This is not right. It doesn't need to be like this," said Jane, desperately trying to keep her voice level.

The plane suddenly shuddered as the undercarriage struck the top of the jungle canopy. Without a hand on the controls, the plane had drifted dangerously low. Tarzan was thrown backward into the aisle and Greystoke gasped for air as he grabbed the stick. But it was too late. Just visible in the aircraft's lights, a single tree rose twenty feet above the canopy around it. The snarl of branches struck the port engine. Most of the branches shredded in the propeller, but the impact was enough to puncture the metal housing of the engine, and it exploded in a billow of orange flame.

Greystoke wrestled the controls as the plane dipped down toward the jungle. Every light on the console flashed and a dozen alarms squawked.

Tarzan braced himself as the aircraft floor turned into a slide. Robbie's unconscious body started to roll past but Tarzan hoisted him effortlessly over his shoulder with one hand. He then ran up the incline toward Jane, who had wedged herself in the last seat at the tail of the plane and was clinging on to the chair in front of her with all her might. Tarzan yanked her up.

"We go!"

Jane looked around in disbelief as Tarzan pushed her toward the door. "Go where? Are you crazy?"

Greystoke wrestled the unresponsive stick and fumbled to ease the throttle down. He only turned when he felt his cousin's gaze burn into the back of his neck. Their eyes met for a second: Greystoke pleading, Tarzan coolly detached like somebody observing an insect.

Then the plane violently rocked as the nose pierced the canopy. Branches furiously whipped the aircraft's skin and shattered the remains of the windscreen. Greystoke ducked behind the instruments to avoid having his head sliced off. He didn't see Tarzan wrap his free arm around Jane and take a running jump through the door.

• • •

Jane hated the sensation of freefalling as Tarzan bailed them from the aircraft. She could only see over his shoulder, and that sight was terrifying enough. The floatplane disappeared into the jungle, fire streaming from one engine. Multiple branches lashed at her. Tarzan's bulk shielded her from the worst of it, but, even so, it felt as if she was being struck from every direction. Wood cracked as Tarzan attempted to land on a bough, but their combined weight and speed broke through the top canopy like a knife through butter.

It was too dark to see anything other than flashes of moonlit cloud spiraling above them as Tarzan attempted to kick from tree to tree to slow their descent. One mighty branch hit Tarzan in the back with such force that Jane slipped from his grasp. She ricocheted through more branches, tumbling head over heels. Vines struck her arms and legs, slowing her down. Several thick liana vines looped under her limbs, almost pulling them from their sockets, but yanked her to a complete stop. Only then did she realize she'd been screaming nonstop from the moment they had jumped from the plane. She closed her mouth.

The jungle was so silent she could hear the blood pounding in her ears. She couldn't hear the drone of the aircraft's remaining engine or the explosion she had been anticipating. Nor could she hear anything of Tarzan or Robbie.

Then the usual insect and frog chorus started again, after holding their collective silence for several moments. The vines suspending Jane creaked as she gently swung in the darkness with no idea how far the ground was below. She only hoped that Tarzan and Robbie were safe too. . . .

13

Greystoke's eyes fluttered open and it took him a long moment to gather his wits. He was alive, which was a surprise, and lying across the aircraft's console. The gauges and dials beneath his cheek were broken and blotched with blood.

He tried to sit up, but every part of his body protested. He tried again, and the aircraft gently swayed around him. His head butted a thick tree limb, and something crushed his left foot, which just added to his confusion.

He closed his eyes, rubbing his throbbing head. *Calm down,* he instructed himself. *You're alive. . . . Ensure it stays that way.*

He took a deep, shuddering breath and looked around. He was lying on the control panel, which meant the aircraft was suspended nose-down from a tree—how far above the ground he couldn't tell. A huge branch had torn the roof of the cockpit off as it buried itself into the plane and was no doubt responsible for catching the aircraft. From his limited viewpoint he could see one side of the plane had buckled, wedging his foot in place. He wriggled his toes and was satisfied his foot was still attached.

Craning his neck, he could just barely see that the flaming engine had been torn off by a fist of creepers and branches, and now hung several feet above him. The orange flame burned fiercely, casting a golden light over the wreckage. Luckily, the surrounding leaves were so damp they hadn't ignited, only charred black as they burned.

A peculiar smell caught his nose. At first he was worried it was avgas—if the plane's fuel was leaking then he could still be burned alive. But it was not as bitter, and was more . . . organic. As he tried to identify the smell, he heard a fleshy tear from above him. Curious, he repositioned himself in his confined prison. Blood was dripping from the branch, running across the instruments. Leaning farther to the side he caught sight of some grizzly red flesh. He was repulsed further when a pale lifeless hand dropped into view as the body above him repositioned. He got a horrific view of the dead pilot whose eyes bore accusingly into his own.

Worse still, the dead man was being eaten by a huge leopard perched on the branch just feet above Greystoke. Its beautiful spotted yellow fur was splattered with blood and its jaws were dripping. Lethal talons tore into the human flesh with a sickening noise.

Greystoke whimpered and slowly moved back under cover. Panic turned his blood to ice and the sudden hopelessness of the situation overwhelmed him. He felt tears of despair coursing down his cheeks as his mind replayed the events that had led him to that place: a lust for wealth, a determination to conclude the work started by his domineering father—a man he had never liked— and the wrath of his feral cousin. All because Greystoke had let his temper get out of control, a throwback to his privileged upbringing, when a tantrum and display of power always got him what he wanted.

Now, trapped in the wreckage of an aircraft in the middle of the Congolese jungle, he was about to be devoured by a wild beast. He wondered if isolated, alone, and terrified were how his uncle and aunt felt when they had met their fate.

• • •

A mile away, Jane jolted awake. She was surprised to have been able to nod off given her precarious position, but fatigue had finally overwhelmed her. She looked around to see what had woken her. The moon had shifted position, a spear of light penetrating the hole they had driven through the thick canopy. Her eyes had adjusted enough to see the pale jungle around her. She could see that she was suspended several feet from the floor and was thankful the vines had been there to slow her from diving headfirst into the ground. Looking up at the ancient trunks towering above her, she marveled that she had survived at all.

Then she caught movement in the foliage. Something was snuffing about in the shadows. She struggled to move from the ensnaring cradle, but her hands were caught above her head. She was a hanging feast for any nocturnal predator.

She freed one hand, which she used to unravel the vines from her other wrist. With them free, it was an easy task to remove the vines around her feet and drop to the forest floor in a near-silent crouch that would have made Tarzan proud. She felt a rock under her hand and lifted it as a weapon as she tracked the sound.

It was coming closer, cracking branches as it did so. Jane wanted to call out, but feared it would give away her position. Another shuffling of leaves underfoot tensed her every muscle. She was ready to spring.

A deer stepped from the foliage, its head raised as it sniffed the air to determine if she was a danger or not. It was almost the same size as Jane, with a pair of short slender horns poking out from its head. It was no threat, but she didn't dare move. Her heart was still pounding from her recent ordeal.

Judging she was not a threat either, the deer continued snuffling the ground as it detoured around her, vanishing back into the trees. Jane turned almost completely around, and was startled to see Tarzan standing behind her. She shrieked, stumbling backward and falling onto her backside, dropping the rock.

Tarzan laughed and helped her stand. Aside from a dozen red slash marks across his chest, arms, and legs, he bore no sign of the terror they had been through.

Jane hugged him. "I can't believe we're alive," she said. Tarzan was unsure if he should return the hug, so just shrugged his broad shoulders and indicated for her to follow.

"Come."

"Where are we going? We have to find Robbie." Tarzan wasn't listening. He powered ahead and Jane had to jog to catch up with him, ignoring the bruised muscles that ran the length of one leg.

For several minutes Tarzan ignored her pleas to slow down as she stumbled through the dark jungle. Tarzan was as sure-footed as ever, never once snagging himself on a root or cracking his head against a low branch. Jane was out of breath and drenched in sweat when they suddenly stepped into a small clearing where a fire burned merrily. Robbie was sitting in front of it, slowly roasting some unidentifiable animal Tarzan had caught for them. He looked up at Jane impatiently.

"Where have you been?" he said crossly. "I'm starving and I'd love to know how one minute I was on a plane and the next I'm sitting in the jungle. I asked him"—he indicated to Tarzan—"but he didn't make any sense. So you better have a good explanation."

As they ate, Jane recounted the night's events. There seemed to be a lot to cover and they both wondered if they hadn't lost a whole day somewhere, but by the time Robbie had explained how he'd woken up on the forest floor with Tarzan towering over him and an aching head from where Greystoke had hit him, it was dawn. With the shadows dispelled, the jungle came alive with the chatter of monkeys and birds, and a sense of familiarity descended on Jane. Now she wanted nothing more than to sleep, but Tarzan refused to allow them to rest any further.

"My family need me," he said slowly, picking his words with care. Since he had started using English again after meeting Jane, his speech was rapidly improving. "The Targarni will return."

"What about Greystoke?" asked Jane. "Is he still alive?"

Tarzan shrugged. "I traveled to find you. Orando showed me the path you took."

Jane frowned. That explained how Tarzan had found them many miles from their usual haunts. She guessed that the pygmy's own jungle telegraph system was more efficient than people gave them credit for, and she wondered how far they could communicate. "Why were you looking for me?"

"I find a woman in the jungle," said Tarzan grimly. Robbie snickered when he saw how Jane reacted to the odd phrase and she felt herself blush. Tarzan didn't notice and continued. "She is injured. May die. Maybe you can help?"

Jane was unsure how they could help, but nodded. "And if this Albert Werper still comes looking for Opar?"

Tarzan sneered. "Then Tarzan will show him."

Robbie sat upright, intrigued. "So it really exists?" Tarzan nodded. "And is it full of jewels and riches like the legends say?"

If it was, then Tarzan gave no indication. He just shrugged and threw dirt over the fire to extinguish it. He stood ready to leave. "It is a place of death," he intoned, and motioned for them to follow him deeper into the jungle.

• • •

Rain battered the fuselage and poured into the cockpit, waking Lord Greystoke. He had no idea how long he had slept, but it was daylight and his stomach grumbled with hunger. He discreetly checked to see if the leopard was still perched on the branch above him, but the beast had gone, taking the partially eaten pilot with it. It could still be close by, but thirst drove the Englishman to reach out and cup as much rain in his palms as he could. Every movement rocked the aircraft and the occasional screech of metal cautioned him that it could drop at any time.

The day drew on and, goaded by hunger and the increasingly dark thoughts that he wasn't going to be rescued, Greystoke tried to free his foot from the crushed wreckage. As far as he could tell, a limb from the tree that was holding the plane's weight had dented the metal. If he pried it away, there was a chance the aircraft would fall. But as the day drew on, he cared less about the risks and began hammering the hull with his free foot. For over an hour, his efforts achieved nothing other than sheer exhaustion.

The rain continued, giving Greystoke plenty to drink. But he was soaked through, and his body temperature started to drop. Seized by uncontrollable shivering, he realized he was going to die out in the jungle. Was it a family curse? Or had he brought this misfortune upon himself? If he had stayed at home at the family estate he wouldn't be facing certain death—bankruptcy, maybe, but not death. Which was worse? His father had squandered the family fortune in order to build an empire. Nothing had been successful. In almost every country they had established a business, corrupt officials set about making crippling demands. The only real success had been the coltan mine, and now that was drying up.

Night fell and Greystoke cursed his misfortune. He cursed his father who had never supported him and his savage cousin who should have died at birth, whose mere presence threatened to take away the only thing left of value: the Greystoke title.

• • •

How Greystoke survived the night was a mystery. He awoke to a new day, weak, shivering, and uneaten. The pilot's pale face had haunted his nightmares. Only, in those fevered visions, the pilot had been alive as the leopard devoured him, pointing a broken finger at Greystoke, claiming him responsible for his grisly death.

Greystoke had been stranded for over a day and any thought of help had long since vanished. He was now beginning to envy the pilot for his quick death, whether it was during the crash or by tooth and claw. A fast death seemed much more appealing than slowly dying of starvation.

Staring up through the canopy, he listened to the incessant chirping of brightly colored birds as they flitted between branches. Their chatter had become so familiar he thought he could pick out individual words—or perhaps he was going mad?

No, there were distinct words. . . . voices. Greystoke gasped as he sat upright. Familiar voices were talking below.

"Nobody survived that," he heard Albert Werper say. "This was a complete waste of time."

"Shut your face," snarled Clark. "Robbie? Jane? Anybody?"

Then a woman's voice, Idra. She had survived Tarzan's wrath. "He's right; if anybody had survived . . ."

They were preparing to leave. Without checking the plane. Were they crazy? Greystoke attempted to shout out, but only a hoarse whisper escaped his dry lips. He tried again, swallowing what little spittle he had, his voice now more of a wheeze.

"Up here!"

"What about burying the bodies, at least?" said Clark, his voice choked with emotion. He was desperate to discover Robbie and Jane's fate.

"This is no holiday," snapped Werper. "We have limited supplies and can't waste time."

"I hate to agree with him," said Idra, "but we've got to think of ourselves now."

"Here!" croaked Greystoke, but his voice was no louder. His hand fell on some loose items of debris that had collected in the cockpit during the crash. One was the fire extinguisher he'd clobbered Robbie with. He hammered it against the fuselage wall as loud as he could.

"Up there!" Idra said sharply.

"We're coming!" shouted Clark.

Greystoke stopped banging. He lay back down, wondering how they were going to lower him down.

• • •

To his surprise, Greystoke woke on the ground feeling fresh and revived. His immediate thought was it was another dream, taunting him with things he could never have. But Clark and Idra came into focus, crouched over, studying him with concern. Idra pulled a needle from his arm and placed it back in the first-aid kit.

"You're dehydrated," she said, as his eyes followed another needle she injected into his arm. "This'll pep you up a bit."

Clark put a canteen to Greystoke's cracked lips, and the Englishman sipped the cool water. "How did you find me?" he asked between gulps.

"We watched the plane dancin' across the sky," said Clark. "An' saw the explosion as you went down."

"How're you feeling?" Idra interjected. "Anything broken?"

Greystoke stretched his limbs and cricked his neck. Everything seemed functional. "Just bruised everywhere," he concluded.

"Where are the others?" Clark asked.

"The p—pilot . . ." Greystoke drifted off as the memory came back. "A leopard ate him. . . ."

"We found the body. He was badly chewed up," commented Werper. The archeologist was sitting on a stack of flight cases, surrounded by Mbuti porters who all watched Greystoke intently.

"The others?" pressed Clark.

"They hailed from the plane," muttered Greystoke, replaying events in his mind. "Tarzan just picked them up and jumped. . . ."

Clark's jaw worked, but words failed him. He sat back with an expression of disbelief and confusion.

"He's not a man, he's a monster," barked Greystoke. "A savage . . . a barbarian . . ." He looked at Idra, studying her for the first time. She didn't appear to show any injuries. "I thought he'd killed you."

Idra managed a rare smile. "Me too. But he didn't, even when he had the chance. He's . . . fascinating. I was wrong about him." She glanced at Clark who was staring at nothing, his brow creased in concern. She shook her head, focusing back on Greystoke. She handed him an energy bar. "Here. Eat. We need to get you back to the camp."

"The camp?" exclaimed Greystoke between mouthfuls. "We're not going back."

"You're in no state—"

Greystoke climbed to his feet, leaning on Clark for support. His legs shook, but sheer determination kept him upright. "We are pressing on." He looked at Clark and, for a moment, softened as he read the sense of loss the South African was experiencing. Clark met his gaze. The optimism and determination that usually drove him on had gone; now he looked lost and bewildered.

Idra offered her hand to Clark. "I believe Robbie and Jane are still alive. After seeing Tarzan . . . nothing's gonna kill him. You know it." She smiled. Clark slowly nodded and let her help him stand.

Greystoke cleared his throat. "She's right. And they will be heading to the same place as us. We must go on."

Clark nodded, but said nothing. Werper smiled and clapped his hands together.

"Good. Let's go!"

Greystoke knew that Clark and Werper were both driven by the same goal as him: greed. He just needed to know how to press their buttons. And he would be damned if he would let Robbie and Jane get to the treasure before he did.

14

With Tarzan guiding them, Robbie and Jane's progress through the jungle was rapid, although they both had to rest on several occasions, as they hadn't fully recovered from their ordeal of jumping out of the airplane. On each of these occasions, Tarzan would disappear, safeguarding the path ahead or returning back with food. Their slow pace was evidently annoying the ape-man and, after vanishing longer than usual, he returned with a handful of nuts. He carefully broke the shells between his fingers and offered them to the pair. To Robbie they tasted dry and flavorless, but as he chewed he felt a surge of energy course through him. Whatever natural remedy Tarzan had found was working its magic. He reached for another but Tarzan closed his fist.

"No more. One is enough for the day."

He was right. Jane and Robbie found their energy renewed enough to plough on through the day. When Tarzan left them alone to scout ahead, Robbie finally had time to reflect on the previous day.

"Y'know, getting arrested by a bounty hunter, sprung out of

prison by a bulldozer, and thrown out of a plane, kinda makes you put your life in perspective. It made me think about what I want in life."

Jane studied him, their eyes meeting. "And what do you want?"

Robbie reached out and brushed a lock of hair that fell across her eyes. "I thought I wanted to go back to the States. Face my stepdad . . . try and get some revenge for Sophie. But what's the point? Sophie would have wanted me to live my life. Enjoy it." Robbie smiled, a mix of sadness and inevitability as he finally let go of the demons that had been holding him back. "I need to live my life for *me*, nobody else. Not Clark, not my stepdad, my mom . . . or even Sophie." He laughed out loud, eyes turned to the heavens as the revelations struck him. "I should thank Lord Greystoke for this. If you can hear me, thank you!"

His gratitude echoed through the jungle.

· · ·

By twilight, they had made camp and Robbie helped Tarzan build a bivouac by bending fallen branches into a shelter and lining it with leafy boughs. It would be enough to keep out any rain, the gray clouds already blotting the stretches of sky they could see through the canopy.

They sat around the campfire eating fruit that Jane had found on the local plants. She hadn't seen the green ovals before, but a troop of monkeys were gathered around them, devouring the ripe flesh, so she judged them to be edible. The monkeys stayed close to the camp, not at all put off by their presence, and their chattering would act like an alarm should danger creep too close.

"How do you know the pygmies?" Jane asked Tarzan as night settled. She saw the puzzled look on Tarzan's face and indicated with her hand. "The little jungle warriors," she clarified.

Tarzan gave a broad smile. "The little men help Mangani, showed me how to hunt with weapons. They taught me skills to talk to *manu* and Tantor. . . . They are friends."

"And the ones we left at the river . . . Orando—is he safe?"

"Yes. Grey-stoke," Tarzan stumbled over the name, "he is no friend of the local tribes. Drive them off their land. Make them work the mine." A dark look crossed Tarzan's face. "And you say Grey-stoke was Tarzan's family?" He gave a short grim laugh; he had seen the plane go down with Greystoke inside. "Now the pygmies are safe."

"They thought Jane was some kind of jungle queen," Robbie said mockingly. Jane scowled at him but explained when Tarzan looked puzzled.

"A goddess actually. They saw me with Numa. He recognized me."

Tarzan nodded. "Numa is no friend of the little men. To tame him needs the hand of a god." Robbie wondered if Tarzan really considered himself in such lofty heights, or if this was an attempt at humor. He couldn't say for sure.

Tarzan quickly changed the subject as a dark look clouded his face. "The others you spoke of. They are a threat to Mangani. . . ."

"Albert Werper?" said Robbie. "I don't think he's a threat to the gor—your family, not like Rokoff was." Tarzan snarled at the mention of his nemesis. "But if he plans to exploit Opar, he could bring others."

Tarzan stared into the fire and didn't say another word. Robbie could only imagine what was going through the ape-man's mind. After all the events Robbie had been through, he marveled that Tarzan hadn't shown an ounce of remorse for letting his cousin die in the airplane. In a way, he envied Tarzan. Robbie had wasted a year of his life dwelling on guilt he didn't need to carry.

As it began to rain, Robbie and Jane took refuge in the bivouac. Tarzan took to the trees, preferring to sleep above the ground when he could. Distant rumbles of thunder quickly lulled them all to sleep.

• • •

The rain stayed with them for the first part of the next day, but the night's sleep had done wonders for them and they moved

ANDY BRIGGS

with a quicker pace. Most of the day was spent hiking up a mountain flank that looked vaguely familiar to Jane. Cresting the top offered a view across a valley and the smoldering cone of Thunder Mountain. There was more gray smoke pouring from the cone than Jane recalled, making it look more spectacular than ever.

"Wow!" exclaimed Robbie. "I've never seen a volcano before. Not for real. That's amazing."

"That's the Savage Lands you're looking at," said Jane softly, a trace of awe in her voice. "That's where we're going."

It took the rest of the day for them to descend the other side of the mountain. The slope was steep and the jungle was packed more densely as plants fought for the rich volcanic soil. They forded the river, where both Jane and Robbie almost lost their footing on the slick rocks, before ascending the jungle flanks of Thunder Mountain.

Tarzan raced ahead, driven by concern, but by the time Robbie and Jane caught up, breaking from the forest to the broad grassland running up the side of the volcano, Tarzan was smiling broadly and surrounded by the Mangani as they welcomed him home. At the sight of Robbie and Jane, the apes gave low coughs of acknowledgment and young Karnath galloped up to Jane, leaping into her arms. He hooted with pleasure, playing with her blonde hair.

As usual, Robbie kept a hesitant distance from the apes. He wasn't completely convinced they liked him.

"So everything's OK?" said Jane as the sun sank at the end of the valley, casting golden shafts of light down its length, making it look breathtakingly beautiful. Robbie was more enthralled to see the dull red throb from the top of the volcano, and the occasional chunks of glowing red rock spit out far above, rolling down the black scree. Even though he was at least a mile from the peak, it was an alarming sight.

"The Targarni did not come. Now you help." Tarzan led them farther up the slope to a natural cave where he'd left the woman he'd saved from the Targarni. She was still slumped on the mattress of dry grass he'd gathered, although the fruit husk he'd filled with water was almost empty, indicating she'd had some periods of consciousness.

"Who is she?" Robbie asked, hoping the attraction he felt wasn't apparent in his voice. A slight head tilt from Jane indicated it was. The girl looked Spanish, maybe in her late twenties.

"I saved her from the Targarni. She sleep all this time."

Jane felt for a pulse, then touched her forehead, mirroring the same actions Esmée did when dealing with the sick at Karibu Mji. "I'm no expert, but her pulse seems a little fast and she is burning up with a fever, maybe." She sprinkled some cold water over the woman's forehead. "You should have brought her to the camp. Esmée would know what to do."

Tarzan looked conflicted. The only times he drifted close to the camp was to check on Jane. It never occurred to him to go there to seek help. He looked across the mountain flank; the Mangani were already heading to the safety of the trees as night fell.

"You don't have to come with us," said Robbie, reading the ape-man's reluctance. "We can take her if you show us the way."

Jane was doubtful. "Robbie, I don't think we can. It's going to take two of us to carry her and we're farther from the camp than you think."

"Maybe we can bring Esmée back here?"

"This girl might not have much time left. If she's been like this for days . . . she might not make it." Jane chewed her lip thoughtfully. The forced hike had tired her out and, as night fell, none of them were in the right frame of mind to make life or death decisions. It was agreed to discuss the problem tomorrow. Robbie spent some time making sure the woman was comfortable before he and Jane fell asleep by the cave mouth.

• • •

A wild hooting woke Jane with a start. Something had agitated the apes and she saw Kerchak gallop past, growling fiercely. The Targarni must be attacking. She had been caught in one such ambush before and had no wish to see another. She jabbed Robbie in the ribs as she stood.

"Quick, get up!"

She ran down the grassy slope among the gorillas, who all faced the trees expectantly. Tarzan was squat on a boulder, his eyes searching for any wayward movement. Kerchak stood below on all fours, fangs bared in a silent snarl. The other silverbacks were spread across the slope, anticipating an attack at any moment. Despite walking among such powerful animals, Jane felt at ease, safe in their company.

Reaching Tarzan, she spoke in a low voice. "What's happening?"

"Something comes," intoned Tarzan.

"Targarni?"

The question was left unanswered. Jane squinted at the trees to see any movement. A morning mist hugged the mountain, giving everything an ethereal look. Glancing up the slope she saw Robbie standing at the cave entrance—he didn't have the confidence to walk among the Mangani. Her gaze was drawn farther up to the volcanic cone. She was certain the smoke plume was denser than when they arrived. Or was it just a trick of the predawn light?

A low rumble from Kerchak made her snap back around. Several figures had stepped from the mist. Her eyes grew wide with recognition.

"Clark?"

Clark froze the moment he saw the line of gorillas staring back at him. His face split into a grin when he saw Jane, but he knew better than to make any sudden movements.

"Jane? Thank God you're alive! Robbie?"

"Up here!" shouted Robbie, waving his arms.

Clark gave the tiniest nod of acknowledgment, but his smile grew fractionally wider. "I thought you were dead, boy."

"Me too," quipped Robbie. He was enjoying Clark's discomfort.

"And we thought *he* was dead," said Jane, her voice leaden as she indicated to Lord Greystoke emerging from the mist behind Clark, leaning on Werper for support.

Tarzan snarled and bounded from the rock, crouching low at Jane's side. Greystoke stopped in his tracks, not quite believing the tableau in front of him. Idra stood cautiously behind, her hand poised to snatch the gun on her shoulder, but she had the sense not to do it just yet.

"This is quite a reunion," said Greystoke hesitantly, then he forced a smile. "Thank goodness. I just knew you survived."

"No thanks to you," snapped Jane. "You kidnapped me!"

"I was trying to avoid him." He nodded toward Tarzan, his eyes never leaving his cousin. "He was trying to kill me."

Tarzan bellowed furiously, setting everybody on edge. "Leave this land!" he demanded.

Greystoke raised his hand to placate him. "Please, we only seek to pass through."

Tarzan roared again, and Greystoke took a step backward.

"I'll make this easy for you," Jane said. "Turn around and never come back, or"—she gestured to Tarzan and the gorillas—"they will rip you limb from limb and there's nothing I will be able to do to stop them."

"Opar's not yours!" snapped Werper defiantly, his eyes never leaving the apes.

"It's not yours either!" Jane snapped back. "You act like I should care what you think." She looked at Clark. "You know what *he'll* do."

Clark nodded and swapped a look with Greystoke. "I really think this is as close as you'll get, mate. To be honest, I think you should head back to the boats. Let me talk things through with Tarzan."

"And leave you alone to find the city?" said Werper with loathing. "I'd rather die." His arrogant expression dropped when Tarzan issued a guttural growl, and he took a quick step backward with Greystoke.

"I think that can be arranged, mate," said Clark tersely. "Better do as she says and think yourself lucky you're still alive."

Robbie suddenly called down the slope, "Wait!" Werper and Greystoke stopped, afraid to take another step. "Do you have a first-aid kit on you?" All eyes turned to Idra. "We need some help."

Idra stepped forward, but both Tarzan and Kerchak growled, the old silverback stamping his fist into the mountainside. Tarzan hadn't forgotten who had shot him.

ANDY BRIGGS

Jane turned to Tarzan and whispered. "Robbie's right, we might be able to save the woman. But we need their help."

She could see the conflict in Tarzan's eyes. She slowly reached out and squeezed his shoulder—it felt like rock. "Trust me. I won't let them harm you or the Mangani. They're my family too."

With great reluctance Clark and Idra were allowed up the slope, flanked by a pair of silverbacks who snarled the entire time. Jane had ordered Idra to drop her rifle, which she did reluctantly only when Lord Greystoke ordered her to comply. Greystoke and Werper stayed put, watching the scene intently, their every move monitored by Kerchak.

Clark and Idra were surprised to see the woman slumped in the cave. Clark's torrent of questions went unanswered as Idra went to work with the first-aid kit. Tarzan watched, filled with suspicion, as Idra drew fluids from small glass vials into a syringe. "She has a fever," Idra said, glancing at Tarzan. "But you've done well keeping her stable." She injected the antibiotics and sat back, gently dabbing the woman's forehead. Idra met Tarzan's stoic gaze. "If it's any consolation, I'm sorry I shot at you."

• • •

It was thirty minutes later before the woman's eyes flicked open and she took in the faces surrounding her. She spoke in Spanish, but switched to English when she saw they didn't understand.

"Where am I?"

"Safe," Clark assured her. "What's your name?"

"Reyna." She winced when she tried to move.

"You're lucky our friend saved you when he did." Clark shot a glance at Tarzan, who still kept his distance. He'd used the word "friend" in the hope it would remind Tarzan whose side he was on.

Recalling the memory, Reyna's eyes went wide and she sat upright so suddenly Idra was forced to restrain her. She exclaimed loudly in Spanish before remembering her English.

"The white ape . . . my team! Where is my team?"

"Dead. Taken by Targarni," said Tarzan with his usual lack of tact.

130

Reyna let out a hoarse emotional gasp at the news. "The woman in robes . . . She killed them?"

Tarzan nodded. Everybody else swapped curious glances, unaware of this new development.

"What woman?" Jane asked.

"Like a queen or a priestess stepped out of time . . ." Reyna looked confused.

Clark frowned. "What were you doing out here in the first place?"

Reyna collected her thoughts. "We were filming a documentary—the legend of the white ape. Following stories about missing people and lost cities . . ." Clark glanced down the hill to where Greystoke and Werper were still being held back by the Mangani. He was thankful they hadn't heard this; the last thing they wanted was the world descending on Opar. "We were attacked. . . ." She drifted off, then looked curiously at Tarzan. "And you saved me. Underground."

Clark was desperate for any tidbit of information. "Do you remember how you got into the lost city?"

Reyna shook her head. "The woman's face . . . I have seen her before."

"That's unlikely," said Jane dismissively. She didn't want people descending in Tarzan's territory either.

Reyna emptied the water from the fruit husk, grimacing at the vitamin supplements Idra had slipped into it. "I could have sworn she was Larissa Dorman, an American anthropologist who went missing seven years ago." Jane felt the hairs on the back of her neck rise and a cold shiver ran through her as Reyna continued. "This jungle has taken more than its share of lives. The British Lord Greystoke"—she was unaware of the glances toward Tarzan—"numerous explorers . . . The local tribes call it the Savage Lands for a reason."

"And you think this Larissa woman is still alive?"

Reyna nodded and managed to look sheepish. "I know how it sounds, but I think so. And if any of my team are still alive in that place, we must go back." She looked pleadingly at Tarzan.

"Of course we will," said Clark, gently restraining her shoulder and not quite believing his luck that the conversation had swung in his favor. "But you're too weak to go. Better you tell me where you think this city is."

Before she could respond, a chorus of fierce bellows split the morning calm. Tarzan's head jerked up. He was coiled, ready for action.

"Targarni!" he growled. "They are here!"

Clark followed Jane and Robbie from the cave and they looked down the mountain slope at a terrifying sight. An army of Targarni swarmed from the jungle. This was no ambush. This was war.

15

Pale apes emerged from the mist like cursed jungle spirits. The silverbacks charged forward, thundering past Greystoke and Werper, who dropped to their knees in terror.

Kerchak collided head-on with a pair of Targarni. The chimps clawed and bit him, but were no match for the gorilla's greater strength. The smaller apes were hurled back into the trees as Kerchak searched for his next target.

Tarzan sprinted down the incline at an incredible speed. The female Mangani and the younglings raced past him in terror, seeking safety farther up the slope where Jane and the others remained.

One Targarni barreled into Tarzan from the side with enough force to sweep the ape-man's legs from under him. Tarzan landed hard on his back and slipped down the grass slope with the wild chimp clawing at his face. Tarzan used both legs to kick the ape off and, in one graceful movement, flipped himself back onto his feet.

With the finesse of a dancer, Tarzan sprang for a Targarni who had his back to him as it attacked a younger silverback. Looping an arm around the pale Targarni's neck, Tarzan drove the beast into the ground with bone-crunching force. He didn't stop to admire his handiwork but continued down the slope.

• • •

Greystoke and Werper leaned against each other in the hope that their combined mass would deter the pale apes. Greystoke looked frantically around for Idra's rifle, but couldn't see it. He leaned forward for a rock just tantalizingly out of reach. A thundering footfall made him look up, just in time to see the slobbering jaws of a chimpanzee as it bore down on him. Intelligence and hatred were burning in its eyes. Its teeth were a full two inches long. Greystoke froze in utter terror. It was so close that he could smell its rank breath.

Then, a blur of movement as Kerchak slammed into the Targarni from the side. Greystoke heard bones break and the chimp fell limp. The mighty Kerchak looked at Greystoke and snorted an acknowledgment that they were fighting on the same side. The Englishman marveled at the power and intelligence before him. He had only seen gorillas confined in zoos, and had never fully appreciated their might until now.

Mist swirled as another Targarni appeared, springing through the air to take advantage of Kerchak's turned back. Greystoke reacted on instinct and lunged for the rock. He hurled it, cracking the chimp across the head, and causing it to slump aside.

• • •

The mass of Targarni throwing themselves at Tarzan was unrelenting. Every step he took into the throng was achieved with a vicious right hook or wild elbow swing as he parted the savage apes. He was searching for Goyad—the leader was there somewhere, but keeping a low profile.

To one side, Tarzan saw one of the silverbacks was down, mercilessly being torn apart by a gibbering pack of chimps. To the other side he saw the unlikely team of Greystoke, Werper, and Kerchak—

all three standing back-to-back to defend themselves from the end-less attacks.

But where was Goyad?

. . .

Karnath raced past Robbie, the little gorilla gibbering with fright. He leaped up onto the cave entrance just behind Jane and watched with the humans as the Targarni attack continued. Jane caught glimpses of Tarzan through the mass of bodies, but the odds were stacked against them. For the first time in the ape-man's company, she was beginning to doubt they would survive.

With Clark and Robbie's help, Reyna clambered to her feet to watch the battle. Her mouth hung open in awe.

"I never imagined such a thing," she breathed. "If only I had my camera. . . ."

Jane flushed with anger. Life and death were unfolding before them and all the stupid woman could think of was her camera? She turned to speak her mind, but froze as she saw a ghostly figure rise on top of the cave behind Karnath. It was Goyad.

The ape's single red eye burned at her, and she could see rec-ognition across the ape's face. Karnath caught the movement and screeched, jumping for safety as Goyad launched himself at Jane.

Jane's breath was crushed from her as she fell onto her back, Goyad's weight pinning her down. Humanlike hands reached for her neck as she tried to fight him off. Goyad roared, a maw full of fangs and dripping saliva inches from her face.

"Hey! Freak!" yelled Robbie as he punched at the ape's one good eye. The chimp shrieked in fury and lunged at Robbie.

The speed of the retaliation took Robbie by surprise and he felt Goyad's teeth sink into his arm. He howled in agony, and was only saved from losing his arm when Clark cracked his walking stick across Goyad's head, dazing the ape.

Goyad shook his head, attempting to clear the grogginess. He had Robbie pinned and extended his jaw ready to sever the boy's throat. Only a terrific explosion from behind stopped him.

. . .

Tarzan kicked one Targarni across the head before pirouet-
ting around, locking his arm around the neck of another, and
breaking it as he tensed his muscles. There appeared to be no let up
in the Targarni's attack.

He glanced up the slope and saw Goyad leap off Jane and onto
Robbie. The sly ape had relied on the diversion. He was going after
more prisoners. Tarzan shook off a Targarni clinging to his back
and took a step forward.

Just then, the ground shook, the terrifying boom resonating
across the valley. A thick curl of black smoke shot upward from the
volcano and the earth continued to shudder with such ferocity that
Tarzan was almost tossed to the ground.

He heard Werper shouting, "Earthquake!"

Every gorilla and chimpanzee bolted for cover. The skies erupted
as thousands of birds took flight. The world was suddenly thrown
into chaos.

. . .

Goyad's head darted around as he tried to identify the threat.
The roar from the mountainside was more terrifying than anything made by man or beast, and he saw his Targarni flee back into
the trees. A dozen chimps sprinted through the knot of humans.
Escape was the only thing on their minds, and the surge of furry
bodies separated Jane and Clark. With a final snarl, Goyad jumped
from Robbie and sprinted as fast as he could for the sanctuary of
the jungle.

Robbie helped Jane to her feet and they both wobbled as the
mountainside trembled. Loose rubble from the peak far above
them avalanched down, but a belt of trees cushioned them. Twenty
seconds later the earthquake stopped so abruptly that Robbie, who
was compensating for the vibrations, fell back down.

. . .

The aftermath of the battle was grim. Two silverbacks had been killed, and a dozen Targarni. Other Mangani were injured and badly shaken after the earthquake. The shock had been so severe that the differences between the humans and apes were forgotten. Now that Kerchak had fought side by side with them, he accepted their presence.

"The volcano's going to erupt," said Jane to Tarzan. "We have to leave the area. This is something we can't fight."

Tarzan nodded gravely, but his thoughts were torn between taking the Mangani to safety and annihilating the Targarni in revenge.

"Wait," said Robbie suddenly. "Where's Clark?"

They looked around, suddenly aware their party was short.

"Where's Greystoke?" said Werper.

Both men had vanished.

"He was right in front of me," said Jane. "When the Targarni . . ."

She drifted off as Tarzan finished her line of thought.

"The Targarni took them."

Jane looked around in despair. "We have to get them back."

"No," said Tarzan firmly as he motioned to join the Mangani, but Jane blocked his path.

"Please! I know you don't like them, but we can't let them die at the hands of those animals! Greystoke's your family and Clark . . . We don't often see eye to eye but he's put his life on the line several times to save mine. I can't just leave him."

Robbie nodded. "If it was just Greystoke then I'd be with Tarzan on this and leave them. But Clark . . ."

Tarzan clenched his fists, undecided. His gaze lingered on his family, the apes banding together to treat each other's wounds. His loyalty was with them, but then he looked into Jane's pleading eyes and felt a rare twinge of guilt.

Jane indicated to Reyna. "And if any of her companions are still alive, we have to do the right thing."

Tarzan looked up at the furious black clouds spewing from the volcano. How long did they have? He had no concept of what would happen, but he had seen the fire rock inside the mountain and could all too easily imagine what harm that would cause if it spilled onto the land.

Jane broke his reverie. "Tarzan?"

With a bull-like snort of annoyance, Tarzan nodded and stabbed a finger at Reyna and Werper. "You. You. Go with Kerchak, find a safe route from here." To Jane, Robbie, and Idra he indicated to the jungle up the slope. "We go together."

Tarzan started to walk back to the Mangani to share his plan, but Werper blocked his path. Tarzan refused to slow down and roughly shouldered the Belgian out of the way.

"Wait a moment," said Werper. "I'm going with you. If you're going to Opar, I deserve to be there!"

"No."

"No? You don't own me, Tarzan. You can't tell me what I can or cannot do! I'm coming with you and that's that!" Werper blocked Tarzan's path again and folded his arms. He wasn't going to be swayed.

Tarzan grabbed the man by the scruff of the neck and, with one arm, lifted Werper off his feet. "Go with them or I will feed you to the Targarni."

The raw show of strength shut up Werper. He grudgingly helped Reyna down the slope, into the Mangani fold.

• • •

It took several hours for the expedition to get ready to leave. The humans required food and wounds had to be tended to. The bite Robbie had sustained to his arm was particularly nasty and Idra had to apply basic stitches to hold the flesh together. A half inch farther and Goyad would have severed muscle, so Robbie was fortunate he still could move his arm, no matter how painful it was. Idra patted his other arm.

"There you go, soldier," she said and winked.

Robbie frowned, wondering why she was being so friendly. He noticed that she kept glancing at Tarzan—each time she looked fascinated.

Idra retrieved her rifle and told Tarzan that Mbuti porters were at the bottom of the valley with the rest of the equipment, which they would find useful on their rescue mission.

Robbie and Idra hurried back to the river, returning an hour and a half later with bad news. The Mbuti had gone. They saw signs of Targarni and guessed some of the porters managed to escape with a boat, but the others—and the equipment—had vanished.

Werper was terrified to be surrounded by the band of gorillas as he and Reyna finally headed down the slope to a new pasture beyond the valley, which Tarzan had identified to Kerchak. Reyna had watched the whole interaction and marveled at how Tarzan was able to communicate with the apes. Werper didn't care. He hated playing babysitter to the Spaniard and had no desire to be any closer to the apes.

Only when the Mangani had safely disappeared into the trees did Tarzan signal that his party should leave. An eerie silence smothered the landscape. The bodies on the battlefield hadn't been cleared. Not a single bird had descended to peck at the carcasses. A free meal was never passed up in the jungle, yet the animals could sense the potent danger of the volcano and stayed away.

Tarzan could sense it too. It was something primal inside him, warning him to turn back as he led Jane, Robbie, and Idra up the flanks of the rumbling volcano, toward Opar.

• • •

The mountainside became steeper the higher they climbed. The rich foliage underfoot suddenly gave way to fine black rock, the volcanic scree that had poured down during the quake and now hampered their progress. For every two steps forward they slid a step back.

The jungle was deathly quiet and only the occasional grumble from the smoking cone broke the monotony of their footsteps. The Targarni's trail as they fled to their lair was clearly visible in the rubble.

Hours passed and they were all silently frustrated with their slow progress. Nobody wanted to be the first to ask to rest, and to everyone's surprise, it was Idra who finally spoke up.

"How much farther?" she asked, panting hard.

"We are close," said Tarzan in a low voice. Jane hadn't seen him so subdued before. When he wasn't being fierce, he was full of the joys of life. Being this close to Opar was troubling him deeply.

They pushed on through tall plants that blocked their view ahead and could only be cleared with a machete. The tough going and the heat wore Robbie down, but the thought of what Clark might be going through spurred him on. He was slashing the foliage aside with renewed vigor when a snarling face lunged at him through the leaves. "WHOA!" Robbie stumbled, the weight of his pack causing him to fall.

Jane and Tarzan burst into laughter despite the oppressive atmosphere. Robbie looked frantically around, wondering from which direction the attack would come. Idra stepped over him and pulled the straggling plants aside, revealing a stone snake intricately carved from a single block. The weather had blunted most of its features and moss had covered other sections, but at over six feet tall, it was still impressive.

Idra ran her hand across the statue in awe. She looked around. "This is it."

Beyond the stone guardian the trees thinned out. Everything was covered in a fine layer of scree, but the avalanche appeared to have bypassed the ancient site. Angular blocks of stone—all that remained of the ancient buildings—poked through the vegetation.

The entrance to the city lay between a pair of carved lion's paws, and a black hole beckoned them below ground. But what drew their attention was above the claws. The faded remains of a lion statue, about the size of a house, had crumbled as to be almost unrecognizable. It reminded Jane of the Egyptian Sphinx she'd seen in pictures, except where the Sphinx had a lion's body, this head had been mounted on the base of a huge stepped pyramid that rose almost a hundred feet from the earth. Soil and plants covered half the structure, but the quake had dislodged the other half, making it look as if the pyramid was bursting from the mountainside.

"Now that's impressive," Robbie conceded.

"Opar . . ." said Idra breathlessly. "Legend says the Oparians worshipped the animals of the jungle." She indicated to the panels between each step. They were covered in detailed hieroglyphs, depicting jungle scenes and fierce animals. The soil had preserved them with remarkable clarity. "They were said to be able to commune with the animals."

"How do you know all this?" Jane suddenly asked suspiciously.

"Albert has been searching for this place his whole life. He met a man who had crawled from the jungle, barely alive, clutching an opal the size of his fist. He claimed to have escaped from here." She looked sheepishly at Jane. "He was part of the missing anthropology expedition Reyna mentioned. As soon as she said that, we knew we were close to finding this place."

Robbie switched on a flashlight and shone it into the depths of the entrance. "We're going in there?" he said anxiously.

"You're not claustrophobic are you?" Jane teased, although she was feeling less than bullish at the prospect herself. Robbie gave her a look that suggested he didn't want to find out.

The ground suddenly trembled. It was not as severe as earlier, but this close to the cone, the noise sounded more terrible than ever. It only lasted for seconds but it was enough to unnerve them all.

"Are you sure the Targarni took Clark in there?" Robbie asked, shining his light back in the cave. Tarzan nodded, and Robbie frowned. "Looks like something is moving—" He was cut off as thousands of bats suddenly blasted from the cave. The squeals and fluttering wings zipped past them all, forcing everybody to crouch, arms wrapped tightly over their heads.

Idra screamed, but Jane had enough presence of mind to keep it together. She found it incredible that not a single bat hit them, such were their navigational skills. The group looked up to see the sky had turned black as thousands of bats obscured the sun. With the broiling volcano so close, Jane wouldn't have been surprised to discover they had reached the end of the world.

"Let's get this over with," said Robbie, trying to mask his anxiety. He took a deep breath, and led the group into the cave. Into the depths of Opar.

16

Kerchak rapidly led the band through the jungle, easily descending down steep grassy ravines that had Werper and Reyna slipping on their backsides as they ungracefully followed the apes. When they reached the river, the procession of apes continued onward without slowing. The two humans slowed the party down, but Werper walked ahead of Reyna now that she was fit enough to walk on her own. His thoughts went back to Opar and the dying man who had crawled from the jungle with incredible evidence of the lost city.

Werper had been trawling through a small village market on the off chance that something of archeological significance had made it out of the jungle. In the past he had been handed several intriguing trinkets that hinted at a lost civilization, discovered by poachers venturing deep into the bush. This time he heard tales of a dying westerner who had been saved by a nun and lived in a small Christian church on the edge of the village. Werper lied his way in to seeing the man, claiming to be a member of a search party looking for him.

The man was in a malarial daze as he wove his tale, even secretly sharing the opal, exquisitely embellished with a snake, that he'd found. Luckily for Werper, the nun had left for water so she did not see the exchange. He had precious seconds to decide what to do next. The man was unlikely to recover, and Werper couldn't afford anybody else hearing the stories. . . . So he pressed a pillow across the man's face. The man was too weak to struggle against the attack, and when the nun returned, Werper broke the sad news of the man's passing away.

Even with the new evidence, going to Lord Greystoke was the only viable option Werper had left. He had spoken to Greystoke's father on a number of occasions as he tried to obtain the geological survey of the area that Tarzan's parents had gathered. They had believed in the Opar legend too, and rumor had it that they'd found the site, but when Werper learned of their plane crash he concluded that angle was a lost cause.

However, his tales of treasure stayed with Greystoke, and when he inherited the title, Werper suddenly had access to the resources he needed. He was closer than ever to finally locating the civilization that would etch his name in the history books, and the wealth, which would wash away all his worries. All he needed were the Claytons' maps of the area.

Years ago, a Frenchman named D'Arnot had emerged from the wilderness saying he had found the rightful heir to Greystoke living in the jungle. Werper concluded that if a son had survived, then there must still be aircraft wreckage. The previous Lord Greystoke had publicly discredited D'Arnot, and the Frenchman vanished before Werper could question him.

When William Greystoke revealed that a group of loggers claimed to have found the aircraft, it was the last piece of the jigsaw Werper needed. It was as if fate had orchestrated events for him to find Opar so he could reveal it to the world. But now he was being forced to walk in the opposite direct after being so teasingly close to it.

Kerchak selected a shallow area of the river rapids to cross, and the Mangani followed in single file. Werper and Reyna were the last to cross. Reyna used a sturdy branch to help keep her balance on the slick rocks. Werper watched her carefully pick her route while the apes continued on ahead without waiting for them.

Werper looked longingly behind. He could just see the smoldering volcano teetering over the treetops—a beacon signifying his thwarted ambition. He glanced at Reyna, who wobbled as she fought to keep her balance in the fast-flowing river. He'd be damned if he was going to play babysitter and turn his back on his dreams. Without making a conscious decision, Werper turned back and scrambled up the slope. He heard Reyna shout his name, but he didn't care. He would reach Opar before nightfall; that's all that mattered.

. . .

Idra and Robbie used flashlights to light the way. Without them, the darkness would have been impossible to navigate as they descended a wide staircase that curved first one way, then the other.

Robbie occasionally cast the light across the walls, revealing long faded carvings, the grooves filled with moss and fungi. Every few yards there were peculiar circular structures, like archways, that looked like they were supporting the walls, but the tunnel was carved into solid rock and didn't need the support. From behind, it was Jane who realized what the structure was.

"It's a ribcage!" she exclaimed.

Robbie looked around, trying to find what Jane had spotted. "What?"

Jane ran her flashlight beam across the curving tunnel wall. "This. All of this. We're walking through the gullet of a giant snake. That's why it's winding so much."

Now she had pointed it out, it became obvious.

"That is seriously weird," said Robbie in a low voice. He was not enjoying the experience and already found the air cloying. "We should turn back."

"No," Tarzan said firmly. "We go on. Lights off."

Robbie shook his head. "There's no way I'm walking blind through this."

"No light," snapped Tarzan impatiently.

Not wishing to upset the ape-man, the group complied and the passage was plunged into utter darkness.

Robbie laid on sarcasm in an attempt to calm his nerves. "This is a great improvement."

"Stop," Tarzan commanded.

Idra suddenly gasped. "It's beautiful!"

As Jane's eyes adjusted to the bioluminescence, the cave was suddenly, magically illuminated in shades of blue and green.

Robbie had to admit he was impressed. "Wow! It looks like the Milky Way." He reached out. "I can almost touch it."

The darkness heightened their other senses, and they all became aware of a faint rumble emanating from deeper down the tunnel.

"What is that?" whispered Jane, suddenly aware their own sounds would be amplified too.

"Sounds like water," said Robbie. Then, just above that noise, something new, almost like faint voices. "But that's not . . ."

"Targarni," snarled Tarzan. "Come."

He took the lead as the tunnel opened up into a large cavern adorned with stalagmites and stalactites. The Targarni's recent passing had disturbed the path through them and over the narrow natural bridge that spanned the white-water river.

"There's no way you would get me on that," said Jane firmly.

Robbie spotted something familiar discarded at the side of a large still pool. He crossed to pick it up.

"Stop!" Tarzan commanded, but Robbie had already knelt down to retrieve it.

"It's Clark's walking stick." Robbie recognized the crutch Mr. David had carved. "They definitely came this way."

"Robbie!" said Idra urgently as she snatched her rifle off her shoulder and pulled the bolt back, chambering a round in one fluid move. Robbie saw what she was aiming at—a large white mass swimming through the clear pool toward him. He'd been attacked by a crocodile before and suddenly realized his mistake. He dropped the stick and hastily retreated from the water's edge.

To his relief, the creature didn't breach the water, but sank deeper, vanishing into the gloom.

"How can a croc live down here?" he asked with a tremor in his voice.

"That didn't look like a crocodile. . . ." said Jane.

"It can survive as long as there's food," said Idra. "I met a guy once who swore he had seen crocs in the middle of the desert, living in an underground oasis." She nodded to the torrent passing through the center of the cave.

"That doesn't sound real," said Robbie.

Idra arched an eyebrow at him. "Really? Then you won't believe it if I told you there were sharks in the Congo River?" Robbie shook his head dismissively. "Bull sharks. They can survive in fresh water. They've even been found all the way up the Amazon. I saw them once."

Jane didn't believe a word of it, and neither did Robbie, but the conversation had spooked him. "I don't want to hang around," he said.

"Me neither," Jane agreed, pushing her fear of the bridge aside. "Let's continue."

As they crossed the bridge, Jane had visions of an albino crocodile leaping out to snatch them away, but nothing happened. They approached another archway in the far wall, and Tarzan motioned for them to keep low.

Creeping to the edge, they allowed their eyes to adjust to the brighter light flicking in the huge cavern. The bowl Tarzan had toppled over during his last venture inside had been moved to the center of the cave and relit, bathing everything in a bright light. They all marveled at the ruins scattered around the cavern, but their immediate attention was drawn to the large stone snake statues.

"They liked their snakes," said Robbie seriously.

Idra squinted as she looked up at the snakes' eyes. "The eyes are onyx. Valuable, I bet."

The entire plaza was deserted, yet the sounds of Targarni grunts and snarls echoed from a set of three archways in the far wall, each leading forty-five degrees away from the other. The group carefully descended the stairs, hunkering low as they ran between the buildings. Idra kept her rifle at hand, flinching at every flickering shadow.

They reached the sacrificial altar, which was strewn with bones—some animal, some more humanlike. Suddenly, Jane realized where stories of cannibals came from. She tried not to think about it and turned her attention to the three archways as they tried to isolate from which one the noise was coming.

"This place is a maze," said Robbie worriedly. "We could get stuck down here."

The sounds seemed to echo, not just from the tunnels, but also from all around the cavern. Identifying their origin was almost impossible.

"There," said Tarzan pointing to the right-hand tunnel.

"How can you tell?" asked Idra doubtfully.

"I can smell Targarni," muttered Tarzan grimly.

They carefully peered down the tunnel, keeping a safe distance behind the ruins for protection. The way ahead was lit by yet more bioluminescence. It seemed the deeper they traveled, the brighter it got. It was getting hotter too.

Then the world shook with a resounding wail as another earthquake struck. The floor vibrated so violently that the layer of dirt and grit looked as if it was hovering over the flagstones. The wall Jane was leaning on shook. All around them stone was grinding on stone. Jane expected to see cracks split open in the walls and ground, but it was solid, immobile rock. The ruins, however, were not so enduring. Stone blocks toppled from positions they had held for hundreds, if not thousands, of years. All across the plaza the weaker structures crumbled into piles of rubble, decimating the history contained within them.

A close, grinding sound made them all turn in unison. The stone snakes trembled before one slowly cascaded into the other and they toppled toward Tarzan and his companions in what felt like graceful slow motion. Driven by gut-wrenching panic, Robbie and Idra leaped one way, Tarzan and Jane the other, as the statues slammed into the floor with a thud so loud it shook everyone's ribcages. Jane felt grit strike her face, and swallowed a scream.

The stone reptilian head missed Tarzan by an inch, and the apeman's shock quickly gave way to a bark of triumphant laughter. "*Histah* not get Tarzan," he muttered.

They had no time to collect their breath before they heard a series of cracks, like ice breaking.

"Run!" yelled Robbie who was the first to spot the danger. The quake had severed several massive stalactites on the roof. They came hurtling down, shattering on the floor. Some were colossal—over three stories high—and once the larger pieces fell, smaller ones rained down in their wake.

Robbie was the first to race toward the tunnel Tarzan had chosen, pulling Idra with him. Tarzan was next, with Jane staggering behind. She covered her head as stones pelted her. Several dagger-sized stalactites smashed so close that she heard them whoosh past her ears.

Robbie reached the sanctuary of the archway and turned back, waving Tarzan and Jane closer.

"Hurry!" Then he looked up in horror. "Move! Move! Move!" He said the last rapidly, his eyes fixed upward.

Jane risked looking up, and in doing so wasted precious seconds. A section of roof directly above her, the size of a bus, was falling away. It was covered in razor-sharp stalactites, which would skewer her before she was crushed to death.

Tarzan slowed his pace so he could reach Jane. His grip around her arms was so strong she thought her bones would shatter. With Herculean force, Tarzan hurled Jane toward Robbie. He then bounded into the tunnel himself, just as the section of roof smashed down, creating a cloud of dust that choked the tunnel.

Then the earthquake stopped. Unlike on the surface, where the noise and shaking abruptly subsided, underground it continued for half a minute, as a bass-heavy echo.

It took several moments for the red dust to settle. Everybody started coughing. Idra broke out her water flask to rinse the dirt from her mouth and passed it around. They had made it through, but the cave-in had blocked their only escape route. They had no choice but to continue onward.

The tunnel sloped down gently and ahead they could see the bioluminescence turn red. Robbie was not concerned about the lighting—he was fighting a mounting panic and talking increasingly fast as he fought to keep control. "How are we going to get out? There's not much point in rescuing Clark if we can't get out."

"We'll worry about that when we find him," Jane replied calmly, although she was finding Robbie's panic infectious. "One problem at a time."

"It's getting difficult to breathe," he moaned, opening several buttons on his shirt. Not that it helped. He was already starting to hyperventilate. Jane had noticed the air was thicker, but hadn't wanted to stoke his panic.

They passed a room dug out from the side of the tunnel, whose purpose Jane couldn't guess. But Tarzan stopped them and pointed. It was filled with equipment. Some was old, scavenged over decades, while some was very familiar.

"This is our stuff!" Idra exclaimed. She began opening plastic crates and emptying bags.

"Anything useful?" said Robbie hopefully.

Idra held up some electronic devices Werper had brought along. "Not really." Then she opened another huge pack. The second Zodiac raft unfurled. The engine was missing, but the pump and oars were there.

Robbie shook his head, trying to be jovial despite the terror he was experiencing. "That's fantastic. Just what we need. What about weapons?"

Idra shook her head. There wasn't even an extra flashlight they could use. Tarzan guided them onward, and with each step it was clear the atmosphere was definitely changing. It grew even hotter and a persistent ambient rumble grew in volume, accompanied by the sound of agitated Targarni.

"We're walking straight into the volcano!" Robbie exclaimed as beads of sweat formed on his face. "I'm gonna kill Clark for making me do this!"

He stopped in his tracks, but Tarzan gripped his arm tightly and spoke in a low voice. "Stay calm. No going back." The simple honesty of the words suddenly calmed Robbie. Taking a deep breath, he nodded. Once Tarzan was satisfied, they continued on.

Closer to the end of the tunnel, they could see it opened into a cavern that dwarfed the previous one. A dull red glow illuminated the far walls, and they all cautiously crouched at the opening, expecting it to lead onto a bubbling magma chamber in the heart of the volcano.

However, they were wrong—they were not walking in to certain death. And for a moment, they were utterly speechless at the astonishing sight that greeted them.

17

The map was damp with sweat when Albert Werper pulled it from beneath his shirt. Since being handed the recovered maps he had never let them out of his sight. He laid them on a broad rock and twisted them around to match his surroundings, aligning the volcano with any other features he could. The only geographic marker of any significance was the valley far behind him, but it gave him confidence that Clark had been correct and that he was on the right track.

Since slipping away from the Mangani he had run and stumbled as fast as he could back toward the volcano. In his imagination, the ferocious Kerchak was dogging his heels, determined to bring his charge back to safety. But in reality, the apes didn't care about him and he hadn't seen a single sign of pursuit.

Rather than retrace his steps to where the ape battle had occurred, Werper used the map to head directly to the black squares that indicated the ruins. At least he hoped they did. As fatigue began to overwhelm him and his legs throbbed from the effort of climbing the mountain, he began to wonder if they hadn't misinterpreted the small markings. Could Clayton have accidentally made the marks? Had he added them as a joke? That family had a warped sense of humor, and Werper wouldn't put it past him.

The forest he was in formed part of the upper belt of the volcano. Beyond that was a wasteland of black stones, then the cone itself, which was discharging more smoke than ever. He could see flecks of molten orange lava spitting over the rim and he hoped that Thunder Mountain was not ready to erupt just yet.

Another earthquake struck with colossal force, sending the trees around him violently shimmying. He expected another avalanche to dislodge from the cone, but it didn't. He also anticipated the jungle coming alive with thousands of fleeing birds and monkeys, but it was deathly silent. The absence of wildlife was startling. The black scree across the ground came up to his ankles, and grains trickled into his boots. In places, Albert Werper felt as if he was walking on the moon.

He was desperately thirsty, but the only stream he came across was black, polluted by the volcano. With the thoughts of fame and fortune burning feverishly in his mind, Werper forced himself onward. He kept praying the maps were accurate; otherwise he would undoubtedly die out there. He consoled himself with the knowledge that he had met a man who had single-handedly found his way out of the jungle. If that man could do it, Werper could too; he only hoped that if that were the case, nobody would be waiting at the other end to smother him with a pillow.

He lost track of time, and when the wind changed direction the volcanic plume obscured the sun, plunging the mountain into an eerie twilight. On he clambered, often on his hands and knees, and he was forced to tear foliage aside with his bare hands. Without a machete, he was slowed to a crawl, but still pushed on until his fingers bled.

Then he stubbed his toe on an angular stone. Werper stared at it for a long moment and then tears coursed down his cheeks, but not from pain. Such straight lines were not a natural formation—they had to have been made by the hand of man. He knew, even before he pulled back the last veil of undergrowth, that his dreams had come true. He had found the lost city of Opar.

• • •

Tarzan gazed at the view across from where they had emerged out of the tunnel and, for a second, thought he had stepped back into the jungle.

The entire cavern had once been an enormous magma chamber the size of a sports stadium, but was emptied countless years ago, leaving a vast space. The floor and walls were rich with verdant plants that had taken root in the fertile soil, but rather than perish due to the lack of sunlight, they basked in the red glow of a huge magma channel that cut through the middle of the chamber. The molten red surface bubbled as it constantly churned, patches of the surface rapidly cooling into black rock before convection sucked them beneath the surface as the entire channel disappeared through one wall. It was fed by a spectacular lava-fall that plummeted from just below the roof, creating a breathtaking sight.

If that wasn't enough, the underground river ran parallel through the opposite side of the chamber, snaking its way through a cave in the far wall. Only a hundred yards of rock separated the two rivers, but they were close enough to raise a gentle veil of steam that was carried high through ancient magma holes in the ceiling, ensuring the chamber didn't fill with noxious fumes.

More huge snake carvings dominated the cavern. Two had collapsed in the recent quakes, but another four rose almost a hundred feet up the walls, carved directly from the rock face. Numerous tunnels ran from the chamber, a honeycombed network of passages leading deeper into the volcano.

The sheer scale of the cavern was only put into perspective when Tarzan saw a large group of Targarni at the far end of the chamber. Foliage had been cleared to reveal the rock beneath and Tarzan finally saw what had happened to the captives not eaten by the cannibalistic queen and her Targani minions.

Several prisoners toiled at the rock. Tarzan counted eight men, stripped to the waist, most revealing skeleton-thin bodies, and three gaunt women. Their nationalities were mixed, but Idra identified two of the Mbuti porters among them. Tarzan motioned to the others to crouch down so they wouldn't be spotted.

Next to the prisoners, a massive wooden gantry spanned the entire mined area. It was almost two stories high. A huge water-wheel had been constructed on the edge of the fast-flowing river, powering a series of vine ropes across the structure, on which wooden baskets hung. The crude but effective array of pulleys and winches carried the cleared debris so that it could be dumped into the magma river. It was an operation that could easily support a hundred miners, and Tarzan wondered how many had fallen as meals and how many more had worked to death. A dozen skulls—both human and Targarni—had been mounted as a gruesome reminder to those who didn't obey.

He heard a shocked gasp from Jane as she pointed a finger at a pair of familiar figures: Clark and Greystoke, badly bruised and beaten, toiling with the other captives. They hacked at the ground with rusting metal tools. They were all held in check by Targarni guards. The entire troop had taken refuge here, some snarling at prisoners who paused from their menial task for too long, others looking around the vast cavern in alarm, expecting the next quake to strike.

One of the prisoners—a man captured from Reyna's party—suddenly dropped to his knees and extracted a gleaming stone from the rock. As he held it up with trembling hands, the robed woman who hovered nearby snatched it. Goyad was preening himself at her side.

She held the raw gemstone up to the magma, delighted as the diffused light shone through to play across her face. She spoke, her voice effortlessly carrying across the cave.

"Another trinket for Queen La—you have pleased her!" Her gaze lingered on the stone before she became aware the man at her feet was almost dying of thirst. She gave a casual wave toward the river. "Yes . . . you have earned your drink." The man scrambled on his belly to the river and drank heavily from it. The self-styled Queen La ignored him, dancing almost graciously in a circle as she admired the gemstone.

"She's insane," said Idra in a low voice.

Tarzan could see Queen La had no real power over the Targarni, and couldn't imagine they only carried out her wishes to get the next scrap of succulent human flesh. She had to have some other form of control. He could only guess that La had trained them to be accustomed to eating human flesh; otherwise they would have ripped her limb from limb the moment she stepped foot in Opar.

Jane moved to get a better view. "How do we free them?" They couldn't see any chains or ropes binding the prisoners, so they were held by fear alone. Fear could do terrible things to a man's mind and Tarzan imagined they had seen plenty of cannibalistic rituals, which made them frightened for their own lives.

There were more than twenty Targarni, still overwhelming odds even if there were twice as many humans, but a plan formed in Tarzan's mind. Goyad had employed a diversion strategy several times and Tarzan wondered if the ape would fall for his own trick. There was only one way to find out.

"Be ready," said Tarzan as he ran silently from the tunnel and disappeared into the dense foliage.

"Be ready for what?" hissed Jane. But Tarzan had disappeared.

• • •

Every fiber in Lord Greystoke begged to sit and rest, though he didn't dare; instead, he lifted a rusting pickaxe and feebly struck the rock—any harder and either the metal would snap or he would. Some of the tools they had been given were over a century old, harkening back to when Belgium had occupied the country. Others were new, stolen from some poor souls captured for the hellish task.

Both he and Clark had been abducted when the Targarni fled the earthquake. He was sure they hadn't been targeted—they were just the unfortunate victims who had been in the apes' path. Those last few seconds of freedom had replayed through his mind as they were carried to the city, and each time the image of Werper pushing Greystoke in front of himself as a human shield magnified in his mind. There was no doubt about it: the weasel had sacrificed Greystoke to save his own skin.

The apes had dumped them on the sacrificial altar when they arrived. Greystoke and Clark hadn't realized what it was at the time, only noticing it was covered in thick dried blood. Greystoke had been convinced they were about to be ripped apart, but their fate was spurred by the arrival of a hauntingly familiar face: Larissa Dorman. He had recognized the missing anthropologist from photos he and Werper had gathered while researching Opar. He had been quite taken by the photo of the young brunette with a winning smile and sparkling eyes. But in reality she was a very different creature.

Referring to herself in the third person as Queen La, it was immediately clear the years of isolation had driven her mad. The beauty whom Greystoke had seen in the photographs was now a cold unsmiling woman who had woven glowing lichen into her hair. Her skin had turned so pale the blue veins on her forehead were visible. Yet a trace of her former beauty held out—until she smiled. It chilled Greystoke to the core. She had filed her teeth down to jagged fangs that made her look inhuman.

Despite her sinister appearance, Greystoke could not stop his gaze from being drawn toward the precious gems that had been crudely sewn into her patchwork robe, constructed from the clothes of past victims. In the low light, the gems glittered tantalizingly. He had no doubt their worth was incalculable.

Clark had tried to reason with the queen, but his words only drew more scorn until she toyed an ornamental sword over his body and he gave up. The silver gem-studded blade was worth a small fortune, but the thought of a sudden death focused the men's minds. However, they were not to be sacrificed, and a horde of growling apes led them deeper into the city. They could only wonder what fate had in store for them.

They had been shocked when, assigned to the mining detail, they had encountered other people. Their expressions were hollow, their spirits crushed. Greystoke soon discovered that talking brought angry punches from the Targarni guards, as did stopping to rest. All the while, Queen La would strut around the cavern, keenly watching the workers one minute, then reminiscing in some crazed daydream the next.

One man, an Indian, had fallen to his knees in despair when the new prisoners were brought in. He threw down his pickaxe and hurled himself at Queen La. The albino ape intercepted the attack and delivered swift punishment by stunning the man. Any horrific punishment Greystoke could imagine paled into insignificance when Queen La began eating the unconscious, but still live, man, her pointed teeth effortlessly slicing through the flesh. She tossed raw meat to the Targarni, who clamored like hoodlums to get their share.

Only Greystoke and Clark watched the macabre spectacle, unable to tear their horrified gazes away. The other workers had seen it all too often and averted their eyes from the fate they all ultimately shared. No wonder shackles weren't needed to keep the prisoners in check. Working yourself to death was a much more civilized way to go.

As Greystoke hacked at the ground, he suddenly realized the black material was not just volcanic rock. He knelt, feeling the texture—it was a huge deposit of coltan. The entire area was rich with it. Near the riverbank he could easily sluice it up with his hand. He let out a dry chuckle. Queen La was mining the area for a few precious stones, most of which had no doubt been plundered by the Oparians and lost to history, when the rocks around them contained something far more valuable.

One of the newer prisoners risked punishment by occasionally speaking in whispers to find information about the outside world. Greystoke learned his name was Ramón and he was the cameraman on Reyna's team. He was relieved to learn Reyna had survived her ordeal, although news of the active volcano immediately dampened any hopes he harbored of escape.

When Greystoke saw Tarzan crouching on a rocky outcrop, he thought he was hallucinating from the sulphuric fumes rising from the magma river. The ape-man was concealed from the Targarni by the broad-leafed plants. For a moment, the cousins' gazes met and Greystoke understood his life was in the hands of somebody both he and his father would rather have seen dead. Despite his fatigue, he felt a jolt of hope that he may be saved.

Greystoke quickly looked away, focusing on the ground, when a Targarni knuckled past and barked a warning at him. He struck the ground with renewed enthusiasm and was surprised to see a chunk of rock split away, revealing a gleaming opal beneath. Greystoke reached for it, then hesitated. If he didn't reveal his finding then the greedy Queen La would be denied the trinket and he could at least keep it for himself. He innocently placed his foot over the gem and struck rock a little farther away.

• • •

Jane, Robbie, and Idra edged away from the tunnel, hiding behind a large knot of ferns growing on a porous boulder. They had moved just in time, a Targarni barreled past them and into the tunnel they had just vacated. Moments later, the ape returned, hooting loudly—the cave-in had been discovered. Goyad galloped across to check on the tunnel himself.

As they watched, Idra whispered, "Watch what they do next. They must know which other tunnels lead out of here."

Goyad returned, hooting a series of calls, which sent several Targarni scattering to different tunnels across the cavern.

"I don't think they have another way out," said Jane in confusion, as some of the apes reappeared and checked different tunnels.

"We're trapped," said Robbie desperately, once again fighting to keep calm. Jane squeezed his hand, which had a surprisingly sobering effect.

"We'll get out. Somehow." She smiled.

Jane spotted Tarzan crabbing around the Targarni perimeter as he inched closer to the old mining gantry supporting the water-wheel. He drew his knife and gracefully vaulted up the wooden supports so he could reach the wheel's axle. Propping himself in the framework, he began hacking at the rope securing it in place.

Jane tried to think ahead. Would the waterwheel cause enough of a distraction for the prisoners to make a bid for freedom? With some of the apes missing as they checked the tunnels, this was the ideal opportunity—but she still didn't know how they would escape.

Tarzan slashed the waterwheel's bonding ropes on one side and the entire structure wobbled as he set about severing the others. With a loud crack the waterwheel suddenly spun off the poles that held it in place.

It was turning with such momentum that the wheel shot off at speed, crashing through part of the poorly constructed gantry, sections of which collapsed in its wake. The startled Targarni looked around in surprise as the wheel rolled toward them. One was too slow in his attempt to outrun it and was crushed under the heavy wood.

The prisoners yelled in surprise and dashed in different directions as the wheel passed through the area they were mining. Queen La watched with dismay as further sections of the gantry collapsed, the pulley system snapping, sending buckets of rock crashing to the ground. One crushed a Targarni; another almost killed Ramón, who darted aside just in time.

Greystoke grabbed Clark by the shoulder as he tried to run, and twisted him around to face Tarzan. "Clark! This way." He stopped to remove his gem from the rock as they ran toward Tarzan, slipping it inside his pocket.

· · ·

Queen La watched the stray wheel ramp over the edge of the magma lake before splashing into the liquid rock. The entire wooden frame ignited as it sank rapidly. She turned quickly and saw Tarzan standing on the remains of the gantry, grinning mischievously.

"Get him!" she roared, pointing at the ape-man.

A Targarni close to her hissed with frustration and clawed irritably at her, showing Tarzan that her control of the apes was tenuous. She backed up her command with a short leather whip concealed in

the folds of her robe. The black leather snapped across the belliger-
ent ape. "I said, get him!" repeated Queen La in a roaring hiss. The
ape leaped into action.

Tarzan saw Greystoke and Clark running toward him, along
with two of the other prisoners. But under Queen La's oppressive
command, a pair of Targarni overcame their confused fear and followed close behind, ready to charge the ape-man.

With a bull roar, Tarzan dived from the gantry, soaring over
Greystoke and Clark to block the path of the attacking Targarni.
Tarzan raised his blade and brought it down across the lead ape,
killing it instantly. The second ape was already airborne. A loud
gunshot echoed through the chamber and the ape slumped, falling
dead at Tarzan's feet.

Queen La snarled, bearing her sharpened fangs. She quickly
glanced around, searching for the source of the gunshot, before
turning back to Tarzan who was advancing toward her, blood dripping from his knife.

Goyad suddenly jumped from a rocky outcrop, aiming straight
for Tarzan's back. But the ape-man had been anticipating the move
and had deliberately left himself open for attack. He turned as
Goyad landed on him, sending them both rolling across the rocks.
The albino screeched as Tarzan rammed the blade into his chest. He
had been aiming for the heart, but missed by an inch and the blade
sank up to the hilt. It was a terrible wound, but not the killing stroke
Tarzan had intended.

Greystoke and Clark stopped in their tracks as they saw Tarzan
fall. Clark limped back.

"Where are you going?" called Greystoke.

"We've got to help him!" yelled Clark, fueled by thoughts of
revenge against the mad queen.

Greystoke dithered as more Targarni emerged from the tunnels
they had been exploring and set out to circle the fleeing prisoners.

Tarzan pushed Goyad off of him, the injured ape clutching at
the knife in his chest as he swayed drunkenly. Tarzan rolled to his
feet just as another three Targarni mobbed him, pressing his face
down on the rock. He felt their teeth bite and claws scratch, but he

endured the pain with grim determination, refusing to show any weakness. But they had him prone on the floor, and yet another three apes weighed him down. The loss of blood weakened him and he was unable to muster the strength to hurl the apes off.

A cold cackling stopped him from struggling. He tried to look up, but could only see Queen La's calloused bare feet and the glint of the jewels adorning the hem of her robe.

"It seems Queen La has the wild man as her new pet." She knelt down so he could see her cruel face. She smiled, revealing those wicked teeth. "And she wonders what a Jungle God would taste like."

18

Albert Werper pressed further into the underground laby-rinth of Opar, guided by the natural illumination. With each step, he began to doubt the tales of untold riches and tried to imagine who had plundered the city before him; at least the archeo-logical value of the site was something that couldn't be taken from him. That alone would secure his place in the history books.

Lost in his musings, he almost walked into a pale Targarni that galloped up the corridor toward him. The ape hadn't seen him, giv-ing him scant seconds to push himself flat against the wall, hidden behind a carved rib. He held his breath, hoping the ape would sim-ply walk past.

Then a distant crash and shriek reverberated down the tunnel and the Targarni skidded to a halt, its head cocked back the way it had come, before it quickly turned and retreated back down the passage. Werper breathed out in relief and crept down the passage-way, noticing the light ahead.

The passage gave way to a large balcony area some twenty feet above the huge cavern. His mind raced as he took in the peculiar image. The lava-fall cascaded to one side—the river was nearer to him—and a lush slice of jungle carpeted the floor, just reaching the top of the balcony he was standing on. Below, he saw the Targarni circling a group of bedraggled captives and he immediately identified Greystoke and Clark among them.

He was shocked to see a slender handsome woman flanked by Targarni. The albino ape sat to one side, bleeding from a chest wound as it slid out a knife that was buried deep in its flesh. But all eyes were on Tarzan as he was hauled to his feet by the apes, his hands firmly tied behind his back. As the woman moved he realized her robe was laced with precious gems, and his greedy eyes widened as he watched, unseen in the shadows.

• • •

Tarzan struggled against the rope, but Queen La had tied him securely, looping it around his arms, legs, and neck, so every time he moved he choked himself. She studied him curiously.

"What are you?"

"Tarzan," he growled. "Free us or you *will* die."

Queen La's head tilted back as she laughed, almost pleasantly. "You dare threaten Queen La, Priestess of Opar?" She gestured around the cavern.

The mountain suddenly rumbled and Tarzan enjoyed watching her momentary flicker of concern. She recovered, yelling "Silence!" at the Targarni who had begun hooting anxiously. The apes fell silent, prompted by a lazy swish of her whip. She circled Tarzan as a cat would play with its next meal.

"You come to Opar to free your friends . . . but there is no escape from here. The slaves volunteer their lives for their queen." She gestured toward them with the whip, then squeezed Tarzan's broad shoulders. "You wouldn't even make a meal—all muscle and gristle, no doubt. So if you don't make a meal . . . then you must make an example." She whispered the last thoughtfully. "Yes . . . a sacrifice to the Fire God . . ."

She looked around the cavern, her eyes suddenly wide and

raised her hands and shouted. "Tarzan shall be sacrificed to appease the Fire God!"

The statement excited the Targarni who began whooping their approval. Tarzan struggled at his bonds, choking himself so tightly he dropped to his knees, gasping for breath. Queen La stood over him and mocked him.

"So full of power, Tarzan will make a fine sacrifice once subdued." She crossed to a new section of the cavern—a section the Targarni kept a noticeable distance from. Tarzan was feeling weak due to his wounds and lack of oxygen. With his head bowed, his eyes followed Queen La to a large square bath carved into the stone. Covered in hieroglyphs, it was the size of a small swimming pool and came up to her waist. A large stone snake arced from the end, curved so it peered down into the bath.

Queen La slowly reached in, a manic look in her eyes. With a smile she suddenly pulled out the largest *histah* Tarzan had ever seen. The snake was as wide as his arm and the length of two men. Queen La held it just behind its head, but it hissed furiously as it thrashed. Despite her wiry frame, the queen was incredibly strong—able to lift the snake out with one hand, draping it around her neck and under one arm. The thrashing reptile curled its body around her. She approached Tarzan with slow methodical footsteps, extending the snake toward him. Tarzan recoiled, but the simple act forced the rope to crush his neck. Queen La teased the snake close to his face, which only irritated the serpent. Its jaws hyperextended as it hissed.

Tarzan could see venom dripping down the two-inch fangs and he tried to move again, but Queen La shoved the reptile closer and in a blur of movement it struck Tarzan's shoulder.

. . .

Jane's hand crossed her mouth to prevent her from screaming aloud as the snake bit into Tarzan. The mighty ape-man slumped face-first onto the ground.

"He's dead!" She could hardly get the words out.

Idra placed a consoling hand on her shoulder and shook her head. "Not yet he's not. It's a Gaboon viper. Only I've never seen one so big. It'll pack a punch with its venom. Those fangs sink deep but will have trouble getting through that much muscle. Plus he's tied up so his circulation is restricted. With luck, he could still make it."

They watched as Goyad crossed to the unconscious ape-man. Walking on all fours was painful, so the chimp stood on two legs, as if mocking Tarzan, and kept one hand clamped across its chest to stem the blood from its wound. He sat at Tarzan's head, batting him with a backhand, and tensing to flee just in case the man retaliated. But Tarzan remained motionless. Goyad was about to strike again when a scent suddenly caught his nose. He looked around quickly, trying to identify it.

"We don't have any luck," intoned Robbie as Goyad disappeared into the bushes.

"In that case, he's got about five minutes so I can administer an anti-venom." Idra patted the first-aid kit in her pack. "It's a generic one, but we can only hope it's enough."

"I don't think we have five minutes," said Robbie urgently. "And I hope you can do it without us being spotted."

•   •   •

Queen La began strapping Tarzan to sections of wood that had fallen from the gantry. Clark took a step forward, but a hiss from a Targarni made him quickly retreat.

"We've got to do something," he said to Ramón and Greystoke, but both men looked helpless now that their one chance of escape had been thwarted.

La pushed a plank under Tarzan's armpits, so the back of his neck braced it in place. She attached a rope and ordered several Targarni to heave on the pulleys to lift Tarzan several feet off the ground.

The cavern shook as she did so, debris raining from the ceiling. The lava-fall spluttered, and then spectacularly ejected even more molten rock into the river below. The edge of the lava tube, from which it flowed, crumbled from the pressure building behind. The Targarni looked around fearfully, but Queen La's words prevented them from fleeing.

"We hear you Mountain God!" screamed Queen La. "We will sacrifice this beast to appease you!"

The apes pulled on the rope and Tarzan was hoisted further into the air.

. . .

"Can't you shoot her?" Robbie asked in desperation.

Idra lined the crazed woman in her sight and nodded. "Sure. But then who will hold the apes back?" She lowered the rifle. "And where are we going to go?" her voice quivered fearfully. "Sorry, guys, I just can't see a way out of this." She lifted the rifle again. "But I'm going to take her out anyway."

With the pulleys working, Tarzan was inched closer to the magma.

"Stop!" said Jane suddenly, pushing Idra's barrel down. "Can you shoot the rope?"

Idra looked uncertain. "If I miss, it's not going to be a pretty sight. . . ."

Jane felt anger well up inside her. She was not going to give in, not now—not this close to rescuing Clark and Greystoke. Then an idea formed, born out of desperation. Usually, she would have never given it another thought. But it was their only chance.

. . .

Clark tensed as Tarzan was hoisted several feet over the magma. The terrific heat was scalding the ape-man's legs, but still he remained unconscious. Only the slight rise and fall of his chest convinced Clark that he was still alive.

Clark couldn't see a way out of their predicament, and he had been in many tight spots in his life. He didn't want to accept that his greed had helped lead them all to certain death, it was not a burden he wished to carry to the grave. If he was going to go out, it would be on his terms. He braced himself, ready to run the fifty yards to the crazed woman. Four Targarni blocked the way, but Clark was determined to fight to the death.

• • •

From his vantage point, Werper could see everything play out beneath him. He saw Jane dash from cover, crouching through the foliage just as another huge spurt of magma increased the flow of the molten fall.

The wood to which Tarzan was strapped was starting to char and he could only guess what it would be like for the ape-man to be cooked alive. Queen La and the Targarni watched with glee, the apes hooting their approval and bobbing excitedly on all fours.

Then Werper's gaze fell to the prisoners where Clark was clearly tensing for action. Werper knew the lame fool wouldn't make it a dozen yards. He had wondered how he could reach the queen himself so he could rip the jewels from her robe. His initial plan of waiting until she slept was in jeopardy now that the lava flow had increased. Since everybody was focused on Tarzan, nobody had noticed the magma river was rising. Even as Werper watched, the liquid inched above the channel it had carved over hundreds of years. It was just a matter of time before the chamber reverted to its old purpose and was filled with magma.

Logic told Werper to run, but he was too weak and the lure of the jewels was too great. If a miracle occurred, and he survived the inevitable eruption, then he wanted to ensure he was a rich survivor.

He became aware of the hot breath on the back of his neck before he heard the hoarse breathing. His blood chilled as he slowly spun around. Goyad rose from the darkness behind him.

• • •

Jane crawled silently on her belly through the undergrowth. In her pants pocket she carried a syringe Idra had quickly prepared from her first-aid kit. Getting the anti-venom into Tarzan was critical, even if it meant she got caught. She clutched Robbie's machete in her hand. She didn't know if she had the stomach to attack Queen La or the apes with it, but she would find out soon enough.

She tensed, ready to make the run across the mined earth the moment Robbie and Idra started their distraction—but suddenly all was chaos.

A blood-curdling scream jerked her attention to a balcony where Goyad hurled the body of Albert Werper from the twenty-foot drop. She didn't see Werper hit the floor, but his screams quickly switched to murmurs of pain. The albino gave a triumphant yell and dropped onto him.

Jane watched as Clark made the most of the distraction and dashed for Queen La. He passed two confused Targarni before a third one coiled to attack. But before it could, a gunshot cracked, killing it.

Now it was her turn. Jane bolted from her hiding place. Nobody saw her coming and she made it to the nearest Targarni who had paused in hoisting Tarzan to his fiery death. She saw flames begin to lick the surface of the wooden disk, which only served to ignite her own rage.

She swung the machete at the savage apes, closing her eyes as she did so. The blade decapitated one, the other screeching in fear as it jumped back several paces before twisting around to attack her. Another gunshot rang out and the rock close to the ape's foot shattered as Idra's bullet ricocheted from it. The ape bolted for safety, and Jane hoped that Idra's aim would hold steady before she was shot too.

• • •

"No!" screamed Queen La as Clark collided into her. She staggered backward, falling hard, still with the great viper around her shoulders. Clark fell next to her, uncomfortably close to the magma's edge. He tried to scramble away, but the snake was blocking his only path to safety. It coiled, hissing loudly as its head swayed between him and Queen La, deciding who to strike first.

. . .

Robbie could scarcely believe Jane's escape plan when she had revealed it back in the tunnel, but now he could see it was the only chance they had. He sprinted down the tunnel to retrieve the raft from the alcove room. Rolling the raft back into its carry bag wasted precious moments. He was halfway back when all hell broke loose in the cavern.

"You were supposed to wait!" he muttered when he heard Idra's first gunshot.

Emerging from the tunnel, he saw Idra quickly reloading her rifle. She gave a quick nod of the head. "Go!"

Robbie followed the back wall, circling around to the river. Jane's distraction was working perfectly—he didn't bump into a single Targarni. He reached the edge of the fast-flowing river and slung the pack to the ground. As he unrolled the raft he peered into the water. It looked deep and dangerous. He tried not to think about the journey that lay ahead.

He laid the raft flat on the ground and activated the small internal electric pump. It was noisy and he was concerned that it would attract attention. But nobody paid him any heed. He had initially expected the raft to inflate instantly, but Idra had warned him it would take a minute or so.

Another gunshot rang out and he risked peeking over a pile of boulders that was offering cover. He was relieved to see Jane hauling Tarzan back to safety. The ape-man was still trussed up, his head bowed in uncharacteristic weakness.

Robbie saw Clark farther down the magma river, trapped between the molten rock and the enormous snake. He had given his only weapon to Jane and frantically searched around for anything he could use. The telescopic raft paddles were the only things at hand.

Robbie charged from his hiding place, bellowing as loudly as he could. The dozen Targarni around the cavern saw him and galloped to intercept. But their path was blocked by the prisoners, who finally saw their chance for freedom. To Robbie's surprise, Greystoke led the charge, his pickaxe swinging down on the nearest Targarni with lethal ferocity.

The snake's attention was focused on its nearest two victims and didn't sense Robbie. He arced the paddle backward, extending it to its full length in a series of clicks, and swung it as hard as he could. The flat blade struck the enormous snake, and it lunged for the threat, its jaws unhinging so wide the paddle got caught in its mouth. Unable to close its jaws, the snake writhed with such power that the paddle was yanked from Robbie's hand. But his job was done and Clark scrambled away from the edge of the bubbling magma.

· · ·

Jane slashed the ropes binding Tarzan and he slumped onto his side. She put the machete down and pulled the syringe from her pocket. The hypodermic needle was in a protective plastic sleeve and she had difficulty removing it as her fingers were shaking so much. She dropped it and cursed. Taking a deep breath to steady herself, she tried again. On the third attempt she got the needle onto the end of the syringe.

Idra had told her to inject straight into a vein. Jane held the needle over one of Tarzan's bulging veins and hesitated. Even after decapitating a Targarni, this seemed like a terrible thing to do. She had never liked injections, despite her father being a doctor. But with Tarzan close to death, there was no time to lose. She gritted her teeth and plunged the needle into his skin, thumbing down the plastic plunger to inject the anti-venom.

Tarzan gasped and a spasm pulsed through him as the adrenaline in the mixture kicked in. His eyes flicked open and he bellowed so powerfully that several Targarni froze in fear—providing easy targets for the handful of prisoners to pick off.

. . .

The prisoners were fighting the Targarni to the death—bodies, both human and ape, lay strewn around. Robbie looked away, not wishing to linger on the carnage. The viper was still writhing on the floor, attempting to dislodge the paddle, so for now it was no threat. Robbie saw Jane helping Tarzan sit up, so shoved Clark toward the boat.

"We're leaving," said Robbie.

"You're not going anywhere!" snarled Queen La, sprinting to intercept them. "Your queen forbids it!"

She grabbed the whip from her robe and swung it at them. Clark's hand snapped out and he grabbed it. The leather coiled painfully around his arm, drawing blood. But with Queen La holding the other end, he yanked her forward.

"I was never a stickler for rules," he snarled, and punched her in the face, so hard that two of her fangs shattered and she was lifted clean off her feet. Clark pulled the whip from around his arm and tossed it aside.

Robbie tried to help him back to the boat, but Clark resisted. Queen La was not moving. She was lying just feet from the magma, which was quickly seeping across the floor toward her.

"Clark!" said Robbie urgently.

"The jewels!" he said, his eyes filling with greed as he shucked Robbie off.

"Leave them!"

Clark ignored him and approached Queen La. Already she was regaining consciousness.

A terrific bang shook the entire cavern, throwing Clark off balance. The magma torrent exploded in volume to almost five times its size and the cavern wall disintegrated as a huge fiery wall of magma poured into the chamber. Spurts of molten rock landed in the freshwater river upstream, hissing violently and sending up a wall of steam that rapidly cut off visibility.

Clark's hand was just a foot away from the fortune he craved. "We have to go!" yelled Robbie, pulling Clark away from the queen.

The raft had fully inflated as they returned. Idra had made it to the raft and was readying for launch. Clark stopped in his tracks.

"We're leaving in that?" he said incredulously.

"There's no other way out," said Robbie. Already, the steam obscured most of the cavern as it throbbed a dull red, lit by the magma flowing behind.

"Leave everything here," Idra commanded, tossing her rifle and spare ammunition onto the bank. "We have to keep weight down."

Robbie cupped his hands around his mouth and yelled, "WE'RE LEAVING! COME ON!"

Idra helped Clark aboard before following. She reached for Robbie.

"We can't wait!" she warned.

Robbie didn't move and called out again. "JANE! LET'S GO!"

Idra extended the remaining paddle and dipped it into the water. "WE'RE GOING!" she called out to whoever was left to hear them.

To Robbie's relief, two figures emerged from the mist. "You had me worried. . . ." he began—but it wasn't Jane and Tarzan, it was Greystoke supporting Ramón.

"He was hurt saving me," said Greystoke simply. He was covered in blood and his arrogant swagger had been stripped clean by the Savage Lands. A Mbuti porter followed closely behind. Robbie looked doubtfully at the raft, which was built for four people plus supplies—six at a push. He had discussed with Idra how they would get the rest of the prisoners out, but she had simply ended the conversation by reminding him that whoever was aboard first got to live.

"Robbie," Idra warned as Greystoke helped Ramón aboard, before clambering up himself, "get in."

Then Jane emerged through the mist, and Robbie felt one of the many knots of tension inside him vanish. Tarzan followed close

ANDY BRIGGS

behind, the skin on his legs red and raw, but not making a single sound of complaint.

Jane clambered onto the raft, helped by the Mbuti porter who quickly followed her. Robbie looked doubtfully at the boat—it was already at capacity.

"Come on!" said Jane urgently.

"If we board, you'll sink," said Robbie desperately. He hated the conclusion he'd abruptly reached, but it was an obvious one. "You'll have to go without us."

The heartbroken look on Jane's face tore him apart inside. She reached desperately for him, as did the Mbuti man, encouraging him in his Kango language. Tarzan made no move to climb aboard, and Robbie guessed the ape-man had drawn the same conclusion.

"That's it then," said Idra as she leaned her weight on the oar and pushed away from the bank. "Sorry, guys." The boat only moved a few feet; the prow caught against some rocks.

Jane was overwhelmed with emotion and reached for Robbie. "NO!"

As if fueled by her emotions the cavern shook again with a constant rumble. Massive chunks of rock—some the size of houses—fell from above, obliterating everything they struck. Robbie felt as if he was trapped in a meteor storm.

A car-sized chunk splashed down close to the boat, sending a wave that bucked the raft. Idra lost her balance and fell backward into the water, as did the Mbuti man, who pulled at Jane as he flailed for a handhold.

At that precise moment, a familiar challenge pierced the air. Goyad sprung through the mist, his white fur covered in blood. He landed forcibly on Tarzan. As the two titans battled, nobody saw the white shape swirling beneath the water, drawn toward the swimmers.

19

Jane struggled to tread water. The water was intensely cold and she fought for breath as the chill gripped her. She was a confident swimmer, but the current was already tiring her out. However, she thought she could use her new circumstance to persuade Robbie.

"You get on the boat before me or I'm staying right here!"

She had expected him to argue, to tell her not to be so silly. Instead, he stared dumbly at the water. The Mbuti porter and Idra were swimming hard against the current, struggling to get back to the boat. Clark leaned over the side to reach for Idra as she was the nearest.

Then Jane saw what had stupefied Robbie, and she couldn't quite believe it herself. A pale shark fin rose from the water, zeroing in on the swimmers. One moment the Mbuti man was swimming, the next he vanished below the water without a whimper. Jane expected to see a fountain of blood, but there was nothing.

"Shark!" Robbie finally managed to say. "What the . . . ?"

Idra looked frantically around as Clark hauled her from the water.

"I got ya, darlin'," Clark assured her, just as the head of an albino bull shark erupted from the water like a torpedo. Its jaws perfectly encircled Idra's legs, clamping down hard. This time there was a lot of blood as she screamed with agony. She was yanked from Clark's grip and dragged below the surface.

Jane couldn't take her eyes off the macabre spectacle unfolding just yards away. She knew that she was next. The cold water felt like icy pins digging into her skin and she began hyperventilating, barely able to stay afloat, but too frightened to try and make it to the boat.

. . .

Tarzan was still very weak as he wrestled Goyad to the floor, pummeling the wound he had inflicted with his knife. The ape showed no signs of weakness despite the many injuries he had sustained. He was driven by pure insanity and hatred, determined to kill Tarzan, no matter what the cost.

The Targarni's jaws bit into Tarzan's shoulder. Tarzan tensed, absorbing the pain as his other hand grabbed a rock that he used to smash into Goyad's skull repeatedly until the ape let go. Both fighters rolled aside, dazed.

Tarzan had only fought so close to death once before. That had been a long time ago, when he faced the lioness Sabor. He had only defeated her by using his blade and rope, but now he was weaponless.

No, not weaponless. His injuries were numbing his mind. He focused, his hand falling to the vine rope coiled at his waist. He pulled it free and cracked the rope tip at Goyad.

The ape hissed, the vine reminding him of the cruel whip Queen La used to lash her subjects into submission. The ground shook furiously as more of the cavern disintegrated, and Tarzan could feel intense heat as the wall of magma, hidden by steam, oozed toward them.

Tarzan threw the lasso, but Goyad had been expecting the move and darted aside. Just as Tarzan had planned.

The lasso had been a distraction, and the ape had now positioned himself exactly where Tarzan wanted him. With lightning speed Tarzan sprang for the ape, planting both feet into Goyad's chest.

The ape was catapulted backward at speed. He crumpled to the ground, but refused to stay down. With the last of his strength he pulled himself upright and hissed furiously—just as a huge chunk of rock slammed down, obliterating him.

Tarzan retrieved his lasso and ran for the raft. He had expected it to be halfway down the river by now, but was surprised to see it hadn't moved. The rocks had wedged it yards away from the bank. He saw the pale shark shoot through the water, and then saw Jane, shivering as she used the last of her energy to stay afloat.

A further explosion tore through the cavern as the earthquake rose in might. The entire underground city was falling apart. The colossal crashing sound and sudden rush of air told Tarzan they would all be buried alive if they didn't leave immediately.

He picked up Robbie, who started to protest as Tarzan took a running jump toward the raft. He landed perfectly in the center and dumped Robbie to the floor. Their momentum freed the raft from the rocks and the strong current caught it, twisting it around as they were suddenly pulled away from Jane.

"JANE!" Clark yelled, stretching precariously over the edge of the boat, extending the one remaining oar.

Tarzan hauled Clark back into the boat as the shark made a spirited attempt to break the surface where Clark had been hanging over. He threw his lasso with precision, and it looped around Jane's shoulders. She clung on to it with numb hands as Tarzan pulled. It was a gamble—the shark could easily go for the bait—but Tarzan was counting on chunks of rock falling from the roof to scare it away.

The surface of the water became unsettled as rock fell down with increasing fury. A pale fin broke the surface, zeroing in on Jane. With a grunt of effort, Tarzan yanked the rope, bringing Jane just within reach. He leaned as far as he could over the edge of the raft, ignoring the shouts from the others as the boat started to list under his weight. The fin was too close. . . .

Tarzan's fingers found Jane's arm and he hauled her aboard so quickly they both tumbled back into the boat, making it rock precariously as the shark swam underneath. Another slab of roof splashed down close by, forcing Clark to row for their lives.

Robbie and Tarzan checked on Jane—she was in shock, but all her limbs were attached. They looked up and saw the pitch-black cave mouth looming ahead, coming closer with increasing speed as the raft caught the whitewater current and was sucked deeper underground.

Greystoke had wedged himself in the prow and now used Idra's flashlight to illuminate the void. Even with the powerful light all they could see was spitting whitewater as the passage angled sharply downward. The stalactites lining the cave's mouth resembled teeth, and they all shared a feeling of being consumed by the earth.

Caught in the monstrous current, the raft hurtled through the tunnel at an insane speed. Jagged rocks sped past, mere inches away, caught in the glare of Greystoke's flashlight. Clark tried to use the paddle as a rudder but it was a futile gesture. The paddle was best used to push the boat away from the wall when it got too close. It took both hands, so Clark buried his foot into one of the straps on the floor—it was the only thing keeping him on board.

Jane, Robbie, and Tarzan clung on for dear life, with Ramón stowed between them. Robbie's flashlight provided extra illumination, but aside from the wall rushing past, all he could see was the wild grin on Tarzan's face. He was actually enjoying the roller-coaster ride.

The tunnel twisted and turned like a piece of knotted string. Some bends were so severe that the raft rolled halfway up the wall, caught in the frothing maelstrom splashing icy water all over them. Greystoke had stopped yelling in terror when he swallowed so much water he began to choke.

As if the echoing roar of the river wasn't enough to deafen them, the rumble of the volcano rose in pitch. With it the swell of water increased, pushing the raft closer to the rock above.

Holding on for his life with numb hands, Robbie glanced behind and saw a frothing wall of water fill the tunnel behind them, pushed on by the eruption. The raft was riding just ahead of it. He didn't want to imagine what horrors were swimming inside the wall of water. . . .

"HOLD ON!" shouted Greystoke suddenly.

Robbie turned back in time to see a stone column in their path. The raft caught a glancing blow, the rigid hull bouncing off and twisting around like a waltzer. Everybody was thrown to the side, their movement increasing the rate of spin. Robbie's flashlight strobed through a series of images: the wall of water pushing them from behind, the tunnel wall just feet away, the steep dip of the tunnel ahead.

The next drop was so sharp that the raft flew out of the water, the prow crashing into the roof. Greystoke slid back along the slick rubber and Tarzan's hand shot out to stop his cousin from falling out.

The raft did a belly flop back into the steep flume and their speed increased before the tunnel bent back to near horizontal so suddenly that the raft was completely submerged.

The raft was designed to float even if swamped so its positive buoyancy shot it back to the surface like a cork popping from a bottle. Robbie tried to breathe, but the water in his lungs made him retch. The world around him was a confused blur. But then the darkness gave way to blinding light as they emerged outside. Everybody had adjusted to the subterranean gloom so well that even with the sun blocked by the volcanic plume, they couldn't open their eyes—which was just as well.

The subterranean river ejected almost two hundred feet above a river as it poured from a gorge wall. It would normally plummet straight down into a steep picturesque valley, but the increased water flow curved the waterfall farther out over the river below. The raft spun as it was shot out. No longer carried by the water, the raft offered some air resistance. But the occupants were still falling fast.

The rushing air was not deafening enough to drown out the multiple screams of those on board. The gorge walls raced passed dangerously close and the raft prevented anybody from seeing the ground rush up to greet them. It was like tumbling through a nightmare.

The raft splashed down into the river with a jarring thud. A massive wave erupted beneath it and everybody was flung into the water. Robbie was submerged in a confusing swirl of bubbles. He kicked his legs and headed for what he hoped was the right direction. He broke the surface and sucked in the tropical air.

Robbie could hardly believe they were alive and outside. Euphoria coursed through him until he was laughing uncontrollably. Everybody else surfaced and swam for the raft, which had flipped over but provided a convenient float between the steep gorge walls. Even Tarzan was bellowing with laughter, and the others fought their hysteria. Pieces of debris from Opar floated around them, but just served to make them laugh harder.

Only the supersonic boom from the volcano brought them crashing back to reality. The gorge cut around the side of the volcano, but it was so close they could feel the shockwave resound down the canyon as the top of the volcano erupted. A fountain of lava spewed vertically up before splashing down the side of the cone. The top tier of jungle burst into flames as the lava swamped it, rolling down beyond their field of view.

Water from multiple falls continued to surge from the honeycomb gorge walls. It must have been a beautiful sight to behold on a normal day, but now, as the sky turned almost midnight black, it was sinister.

Another boom rattled the land as the volcano fountained again, higher this time, the lava glowing with intensity as it spattered down. The multiple waterfalls suddenly eased as billowing clouds of steam poured from the tunnels.

Robbie was getting uneasy. "I think we better get a lot farther away."

"Help me flip this over," said Clark, who picked up on Robbie's trepidation. He tried lifting the raft, but in the water it was too cumbersome.

Then the steam clouds turned red and glowing lava spewed from the gorge tunnels in a curtain of fire. The water hissed as the lava-falls cascaded into the river, creating more massive clouds of steam.

Everybody started scrambling to turn the raft, but they couldn't raise it. Tarzan delivered a powerful punch, which succeeded in flipping the boat over. They all quickly clambered on board, rowing with their hands as chunks of the gorge wall began crumpling away behind them, issuing more lava. It was only a matter of time before one entire side of the gorge collapsed.

The air tasted sulphurous as a third explosion pounded the landscape. Soft flakes began to fall. For a moment, Robbie was confused and thought it was snowing. Jane held out her hand and saw that they were flakes of gray ash, which crumbled to powder in her palm.

"Faster!" shouted Clark, before he burst into a coughing fit as he inhaled the ash. He splashed his face to prevent the ash from clinging to him.

The gray blizzard increased as they furiously paddled around a bend. This stretch of water took them out of the ash cloud's path and they were able to breathe easily once again. Where the gorge had towered on both sides of the river before, one side now lowered offering a wide pebbled beach that led into the jungle.

Robbie paddled for all he was worth, but suspected their rapid progress was due to Tarzan's contribution. They abandoned the raft the moment it crunched on the stones and then sat down to catch their breath. Even Tarzan looked exhausted. Nobody had the energy to move, even when the gorge wall on the opposite bank, upriver from them, gave way spectacularly and countless tons of rock cascaded into the gorge, blocking it. Magma swiftly oozed from the new opening in the ruined gorge wall, sending spectacular lava falls into the river. Water hissed angrily where the two met, sending up plumes of steam.

Jane tried to stand from the boulder on which she sat, but her legs trembled from the effort and she collapsed back down. Silent glances were exchanged as they all ran through the day's events.

Ramón broke the silence as he stood uneasily and extended his hand to Tarzan. "*Gracias.* Thank you."

Tarzan stared at the hand, unaccustomed to the gesture. Ramón was unsure if he had offended the ape-man, until Jane giggled.

ANDY BRIGGS

"That's not Tarzan's way."

Ramón nodded uncertainly and went to pat Tarzan on the shoulder—but hesitated. He withdrew his hand and simply repeated his thanks. Tarzan nodded once. He didn't need thanks.

Jane met Greystoke's vacant gaze. "So? Was it worth it?"

Greystoke wore a hangdog expression and licked his lips, looking away. Jane switched her accusing glance to Clark.

"I had some of them gems . . . inches away . . ." Clark recalled dreamily. "A fortune . . ." He levelly met Jane's gaze. "But I walked away." He looked as if he regretted that decision. "But thanks for comin' for us." He included Tarzan and Robbie with a simple wave of the hand.

"You'd have done the same for me," said Jane with a smile.

Clark pretended to frown. "I think I did that already on a couple o' occasions."

Tarzan stood and stepped toward the river. He watched in amazement as the water suddenly receded. It was choked upstream until nothing remained other than a wide strip of mud littered with decaying tree trunks, fragments of the gantry that had once been in the Opar mine, and hundreds of madly thrashing fish. Against the background of the raging volcano, it was an otherworldly image.

Jane shrieked as she was yanked off the rock and dragged backward into the bushes, clutching her throat. Everybody looked around in surprise, too stunned to react as Queen La stepped from the jungle holding one end of her whip, the other end wrapped tightly around Jane's neck. Her mouth hovered close to Jane's exposed throat, her remaining fangs threatening to puncture the skin.

Insanity danced in her eyes. Like the others, she was soaking wet, with gray ashes clinging to her pale skin. She was weak, her bejeweled robed was torn, burned, and dirtier than ever, but dozens of precious gems still clung to it. The others could only guess at the ordeal she'd just undertaken to escape from the collapsing cavern.

"You destroyed Queen La's kingdom!" she hissed accusingly. "You upset the Fire God and brought death to us all."

Tarzan strode forward with a murderous expression on his face. Queen La hissed like a feral cat.

"Come closer and her throat will be torn!"

"Release her," commanded Tarzan.

Queen La circled around Tarzan, ensuring the entire group was within view. She stood out in the emptied riverbed, which gave her the advantage of more space.

She stabbed a finger at Tarzan. "You brought this upon Opar! You angered the gods! So you will pay with your life!"

Robbie tensed, ready to use the last of his strength to charge Queen La. He felt Clark's hand on his shoulder, restraining him.

"You won't make it," whispered Clark. "She'll have Jane's throat out in a flash."

The stand off was bolstering Queen La's confidence and she leered at Tarzan. "Kneel before your queen."

Tarzan flinched and remained motionless. Robbie hoped Tarzan didn't value his pride over Jane's life.

"Kneel!" hissed La with venom. "You killed the Targarni. You will replace them. Queen La will tame the beast."

Tarzan was unmoved. "I am Tarzan. I am Lord of Jungle." He thudded a fist across his chest. "And Tarzan kneels for no one."

Queen La hissed, thin lips curling back across her jagged teeth as she drew Jane closer, angling her head to reveal more slender neck. Jane struggled, pulling away, but La was too strong.

Jane's move was a feint. As she yanked away, Queen La pulled her nearer—then Jane suddenly threw all her weight in the direction she was being pulled, violently headbutting the mad queen. Queen La didn't expect the move and was thrown off balance, dropping the whip.

Jane dropped and rolled away as Tarzan pounced through the air before Queen La could move. They fell back into the mud. Tarzan grappled for the woman, but the slick mud made it easy for her to slip from his grasp. She punched Tarzan across the face, then held him back with one trembling arm. Such strength from the wiry woman should have been impossible, but she held her own with Tarzan as they traded blows.

Then a loud booming heralded new danger. Lava pouring down the flanks of the volcano had obliterated the jungle in its path and now appeared on the gorge ridge opposite the beach. The leading edge of the lava was already cooling, turning black as it solidified. But from behind, a wave of sizzling red rock subsumed it and poured over the edge of the gorge in a single quarter-mile-wide lava-fall. It splashed down onto the far side of the dry riverbed and crept inexorably closer.

"Tarzan!" shouted Jane. "Run!"

Queen La ignored the glowing wall of rock creeping up on them. She gnashed at Tarzan, tearing a bloody lump from his arm. Tarzan ignored the pain and, with a snarl, grabbed Queen La around the throat, his other hand around her leg as he hoisted her high above his head.

La thrashed and clawed his head, pulled his hair, and tried to poke out his eyes, but Tarzan shook her, even biting a clawed finger off when she just missed his eye. He walked resolutely toward the lava, then stumbled when a gunshot rang out and a bullet grazed his side. Tarzan almost dropped, but regained his balance, turning to see what new menace had presented itself.

It was Albert Werper. He was almost unrecognizable; half his face was burned red raw, and what hadn't been scorched by magma had been chewed by Goyad. His clothes hung like rags as he emerged from the jungle, Idra's rifle pushed against his shoulder and sighted on Tarzan. His breathing was heavily laboured and his voice hoarse and unrecognizable. "LET HER GO!" he croaked.

Greystoke took a step toward Werper, but stopped when the rifle barrel swung toward him, before settling back on Tarzan.

"Next person to move gets shot."

"Albert . . ." Greystoke stammered. "What happened . . . ? How did you . . . ?"

"Same way as you. After you abandoned me to die." He spat. "Opar is destroyed and all its treasure hangs from that witch."

"Don't be a fool, Werper!" snapped Clark. "If we don't leave now, we're all gonna die!"

"Shut up!"

"What use is money if you're dead?" said Clark.

"IT'S MINE!" Werper shouted.

Tarzan ignored him and limped toward the wall of lava. Werper raised the gun and took aim.

"NO!" screamed Jane. But it was too late. Werper had pulled the trigger.

The shot rang out but missed its mark as Greystoke leaped in front of Tarzan, taking the shot to his chest. The impact was so severe that he was hurled several feet backward.

Werper blinked in surprise and pulled the trigger again. The rifle clicked on an empty barrel. With shaking hands he tried to reload, but Robbie and Clark foiled him.

• • •

Tarzan was oblivious to his cousin's sacrifice. He limped as close to the lava as he dared and hoisted the screaming Queen La high. Her imminent death was just breaking through the madness that clouded her mind.

"No . . . please . . ." she whimpered, no longer the strong queen, but a terrified mortal. She met Tarzan's gaze, and for a second he hesitated, lowering her slightly. That was enough for Queen La. Her familiar mask of hatred suddenly replaced her terrified countenance as she lunged for him. Her jagged fangs bit his forehead to the bone.

Tarzan bellowed, "I am your lord!" And he hurled the writhing wretch into the lava with all his might. He didn't wait to see the macabre results of his handiwork, as the river of lava was quickly advancing.

He raced back to the others, stopping in confusion when he saw everybody surrounding Greystoke. The Englishman was unconscious and paling as he rapidly lost blood from his stomach wound. Tarzan looked impassively at the dying man.

"Werper tried to shoot you," said Jane. She stroked Greystoke's forehead. "He took the bullet to save you."

Tarzan had always relied on his initial judgment of people. He had been right about D'Arnot and Jane. People seldom changed, but he had to concede that Robbie had surprised him, so perhaps it was possible the man who claimed to be his family, who had struck Jane and even tried to kill him, could change too.

Tarzan turned his attention to Werper who was on his knees, arms pressed behind his head by Clark, who was warily watching the advancing lava.

"I don't know what we should do with him, but we can't just stand 'ere."

Tarzan knelt at Greystoke's side and tore the Englishman's bloody shirt open. The bullet had gone through his stomach, shredding the bandages wrapped around his midriff. The bullet should have torn a gaping hole in his back as it exited, but there was no such sign. Tarzan noticed fragments of yellow gemstone across Greystoke's chest. He searched the man's waistcoat and found fragments of a yellow opal that had been hidden in his inside pocket. It would have been quite valuable if the bullet hadn't shattered it into a thousand pieces. The gemstone had saved his life, although Greystoke was unconscious and his internal injuries were no doubt life-threatening.

Tarzan stood and yanked Werper to his feet by his hair, pulling the man close so he could see the terror in his eyes. Then he pushed him away toward the trees.

"Go!" he growled.

Werper looked surprised to be given a reprieve, but he didn't waste the chance. He scrambled into the jungle as fast as he could.

"You're just gonna let him go?" said Robbie, equally surprised.

"Let the jungle claim him," said Tarzan as he lifted Greystoke. "We leave now."

Clark and Jane helped Ramón stand, and together they dashed into the jungle.

. . .

Progress was much slower than they were used to, as everybody, including Tarzan, was exhausted and hurt. They kept to animal trails through the jungle, always conscious of the wall of lava slowly advancing behind them, threatening to consume them if they dared stop for too long. The volcano boomed several more times, but they could see nothing through the jungle's thick canopy.

At nightfall they stopped on a rocky outcrop that offered a view across the jungle. Lava still oozed from the volcano, glowing cherry red in the twilight, but it hadn't advanced beyond the riverbed. Taking the path of least resistance, the lava had moved downstream and left the jungle alone. Jane's nightmarish visions of the jungle ablaze had not come to pass.

The jubilation they felt for surviving was tempered by guilt over how many they had lost. Survivor's guilt, Clark had called it—and he seemed to be suffering just as much as the others.

Greystoke fell into a fever during the night, and Tarzan tended to his wounds the best he could before fatigue overtook them and they all slept soundly.

It was the end of the second day when they finally entered Orando's village. Jane was delighted to see Orando had made it safely home. He and Tarzan took Greystoke to the shaman. Robbie had wanted to watch, but they were forbidden to see the sacred rites performed as they attempted to pull Greystoke back from the brink of death, although everybody was fairly sure the Englishman would not make it through the night.

Ramón had recovered well and marveled when he was told that Reyna had been taken to safety by the gorillas.

"Incredible," he breathed. "To film such a thing—"

Jane held up her hand to cut him off. "There we have a problem. If either of you speak about this, if you tell the world of Opar, of Tarzan, they will beat a path here, and we don't want that."

Ramón was feeling well enough that his journalistic training shone through. "The world needs to know such things."

"No they don't. Some things are best kept secret."

Ramón eventually nodded solemnly as he thought about the loss of life and the pointless drive for greed. He saw her point.

The next morning everybody was surprised to see Greystoke on his feet. He was weak, but alive, and couldn't stop smiling when he saw the others.

Clark patted him on the back and grinned. "Glad you're back on your feet."

"I didn't know you cared," Greystoke said, only half joking.

Clark shrugged. "Well, I thought being prisoners kinda bonded us together." Greystoke nodded in agreement. "Besides, there's someone I want ya to meet. Lord Greystoke, this is your cousin, Tarzan."

Tarzan was perplexed by the introduction. Greystoke just nodded and in a small voice said, "I know. Thank you, John." Using Tarzan's real name meant nothing to the ape-man.

Clark was the one to break the awkward silence. "Well, I just delivered on an agreement, so I know someone who owes me a lot of money."

Greystoke treated him to a bemused smile. Jane looked uneasily between Tarzan and his cousin.

"So, what now?"

The two Greystokes met each other's gaze, and silence descended across the village as the jungle held its breath.

EDGAR RICE BURROUGHS
AND TARZAN

From the day he was born in Chicago, on September 1, 1875, until he submitted half of a novel to *All-Story Magazine* in 1911, Edgar Rice Burroughs failed in nearly every enterprise he tried.

He attended half a dozen public and private schools before he finally graduated in 1895 from Michigan Military Academy, an institution he described as "a polite reform school."

Having failed the entrance examination for the United States Military Academy at West Point, he enlisted as a private in the Seventh US Cavalry because he thought he might still obtain a commission as an officer if he distinguished himself in a different assignment. He asked to be sent to the worst post in America—a request the authorities speedily granted.

The post was Fort Grant in the Arizona desert, and his mission, as he put it, was to "chase outlaw Apaches." "I chased a good many Apaches," he said, "but fortunately for me, I never caught up with any of them."

Private Burroughs soon had his fill of Fort Grant, and after one year he was discharged. In 1900, he married Emma Centennia Hulbert, who dutifully followed him back and forth across America during the next eleven years.

He became a cowboy in Idaho, then a shopkeeper, a railroad policeman, a gold miner, and even an "expert accountant," although he knew nothing of the profession. Throughout this period he somehow raised money for a number of his own businesses, all of which sank without a trace.

Life was dismal for the newly married couple. Burroughs became depressed; his wife, discouraged. Perhaps to escape from the grim reality of their lives, or perhaps to amuse Emma, he would often sketch darkly humorous cartoons or write fantastic fairy tales.

By 1911, Burroughs's position had become so desperate that not even his cartoons and stories could block out the frustrating fact of his successive failures. He even went so far as to apply for a commission in the Chinese army. (The application was summarily rejected.) He also applied for a post with Teddy Roosevelt's Rough Riders, but there were no vacancies.

Finally he reached rock bottom. He was thirty-five years old, without a job, without money. In addition to his wife and two children, a third child was expected soon. He could buy food and coal only by pawning his watch and Emma's jewelry.

While working as a manager for pencil-sharpener salesmen, he used his leisure moments while "waiting for them to come back to tell me that they had not sold any," to begin writing *Under the Moons of Mars*, his first story. He recalled:

I had no idea how to submit a story or what I could expect in payment. Had I known anything about it at all, I would never have thought of submitting half a novel, but that is what I did. Thomas Newell Metcalf, then editor of *All-Story Magazine* . . . wrote me that he liked the first half of the story and if the second was as good he thought he might use it. Had he not given me this encouragement, I would never have finished the story and my writing career would have been at an end, since I was not writing because of any urge to write nor for any particular love of writing. I was writing because I had a wife and two babies, a combination which does not work well without money.

I finished the second half of the story and got $400 for first magazine serial rights. The check was the first big event in my life. No amount of money today could possibly give me the thrill that this first $400 check gave me.

Today, scholars consider that story to be the turning point of twentieth-century science fiction. New editions continue to be published annually throughout the world.

But Burroughs was still a long way from becoming an established writer. His next literary effort, a historical novel set in the England of the Plantagenet kings, was rejected. He nearly gave up but his publisher would not hear of it. "Try again," the publisher urged. "Stick with the 'damphool' stuff."

Burroughs did, and with his next novel, his future was decided. The novel was *Tarzan of the Apes*. An astonishing success on its appearance in *All-Story Magazine* in 1912, *Tarzan of the Apes* brought Edgar Rice Burroughs $700 and a surge of success. Burroughs sent the manuscript to book publishers but was rejected by practically every major company in the country. Finally, *Tarzan* was printed as a novel from A.C. McClurg and Co., and it became a bestseller in 1914.

Said Burroughs, "In all these years I have not learned one single rule for writing fiction. I still write as I did thirty years ago; stories which I feel would entertain me and give me mental relaxation, knowing that there are millions of people just like me who will like the same things I like. Anyway, I have great fun with my imaginings, and I can appreciate—in a small way—the swell time God had in creating the universe."

A torrent of novels followed *Tarzan*: stories about Mars, Venus, Apaches; Westerns; social commentaries; detective stories; tales of the Moon and of a fictional Hollow Earth—and more and more Tarzan books. By the time his pen was stilled, nearly one hundred stories bore Edgar Rice Burroughs's name.

In 1918, Tarzan debuted on screen in the silent film *Tarzan of the Apes*, starring Elmo Lincoln. It became one of the first films in history to earn one million dollars. Since then, fifty Tarzan live-action films, 115 one-hour television episodes, seventy-one half-hour animated television episodes, and three feature animation films have been produced, with more than twenty-seven actors playing the lead role.

Although he joked about the films, Burroughs was bitterly disappointed with the Tarzan motion pictures. Often he would not go to see them. His Tarzan was a supremely intelligent, sensitive man. His Tarzan sat in the House of Lords when not otherwise occupied in the upper terraces of the African jungle. His Tarzan was a truly civilized man—heroic, handsome, and above all, free.

In 1919, with financial security assured, Burroughs moved to California, where he purchased the 550-acre estate of General Harrison Gray Otis, renaming it "Tarzana Ranch." By 1923, the city of Los Angeles had completely surrounded Tarzana Ranch, and Burroughs sold a large portion of it for home sites. In 1930, a post office was established, and the three hundred residents held a contest to find a name for the new community. The winning entry was "Tarzana."

By the mid-1930s, daily and special Sunday Tarzan comic strips appeared in more than 250 newspapers all over the world. Tarzan radio serials thrilled millions of listeners across the country, with Burroughs's daughter, Joan, in the role of Jane, and her husband, James H. Pierce—who had played the lead in the silent movie *Tarzan and the Lion Men*—as Tarzan.

Today, Tarzan television programs and films are shown on an array of different networks all over the world. A Tarzan movie plays somewhere in the world every day. And with the contemporary emphasis on outer space, Burroughs's science fiction writings are still treasured.

In 1942, Burroughs became America's oldest war correspondent, covering stories with the Pacific Fleet for United Press. He returned home from the South Pacific only after suffering a series of heart attacks. Ironically, he was unable to find a suitable home in Tarzana, and he spent his remaining years in a modest house in nearby Encino. It was there, on March 19, 1950, that he set down his pen for the final time.

The last line he ever wrote:

"Thank God for everything."

Burroughs around age ten.

Edgar Rice Burroughs at age sixteen in Idaho.

Burroughs's friends and fellow soldiers, known as "the May-have-seen-better-days Club," at Fort Grant, Arizona, in 1896.

Tarzan of the Apes (1918), a silent film, was the first Tarzan movie ever made and one of the first movies to ever earn one million dollars. The success of the film allowed Burroughs to buy the ranch he named Tarzana.

In 1919, Burroughs purchased a ranch near Los Angeles with the money he earned from the first Tarzan movie, calling the property "Tarzana." As the city spread around the ranch, Burroughs sold part of it for development, and in 1930, his neighbors voted to name their new town Tarzana.

In 1922, Burroughs's old friend, Robert D. Lay from the Michigan Military Academy, visited Burroughs's California ranch. Lay had become president of a large life insurance company.

Buster Crabbe, an Olympic swimmer, stepped into the title role for 1933's *Tarzan the Fearless*, opposite Jacqueline Wells.

Burroughs reviewing *Tarzan and the Lion Man*, the seventeenth book in the series, in 1934. *Lion Man* is the closest thing to a comic novel in the Tarzan series, with Burroughs satirizing Hollywood's treatment of the Tarzan character and even spoofing his own work

Burroughs dictating into an Ediphone in March 1937.

Burroughs, right, and Cyril Ralph Rothmund, his secretary and manager for many years, in 1937.

Burroughs working on a story at his Honolulu office on November 21, 1941. He wrote many stories in this office, and sent them to his secretary-manager, Rothmund, in Tarzana. Rothmund then arranged for retyping and submission to magazine editors.

Johnny Weissmuller and Maureen O'Sullivan costarred
in many of the Tarzan films.

Burroughs with his grandchildren, John Ralston Burroughs, James
Michael Pierce, and Danton Burroughs, in 1945.

Burroughs with Lex Barker, the tenth movie Tarzan.

Since 1912, the Tarzan character has been brought to life in television, movies, newspaper comic strips, comic books, and art. Illustrator Frank Frazetta began creating cover art for Burroughs's Tarzan paperbacks in the 1960s, a period when Frazetta's work was redefining fantasy art.

TARZAN: A TWENTY-FIRST-CENTURY LEGEND

The year 2012 sees the centenary of an iconic figure. One hundred years ago Tarzan first swung from the jungle and into the pages of *All-Story Magazine*. Through books, comics, films, radio shows, and countless television shows, Tarzan left an indelible mark on the public's imagination. Generations still know who he is even if they've never read one of Edgar Rice Burroughs's twenty-six original Tarzan novels. There is no better time than the one-hundred-year anniversary to give new life to the world's first eco-warrior.

To author Andy Briggs, it was clear that if somebody didn't inject new life into Tarzan, the character was in danger of eventually becoming extinct, consigned to pop-culture memory. But when he approached the Edgar Rice Burroughs estate to suggest Tarzan be reinvented for a whole new generation of readers, he was astonished by the estate's overwhelmingly enthusiastic response. They agreed it was time for a contemporary Tarzan.

With the estate's blessing, Briggs was given rein to bring Tarzan into the twenty-first century. Everything we know and love about the character has been maintained: He's still an English lord raised in the wild by apes, and he's often a wild untamable savage. But gone are the clichéd native tribes, replaced by warring rebel guerrillas. Jane is no longer an inactive damsel in distress; she's now a modern teenager who proves herself more than a match for the Lord of the Jungle. And Tarzan himself is not only Lord of the Jungle, but also a symbol for all that is good and noble, and for the preservation of the wild, untamable regions of our natural world.

Andy Briggs, author of the latest Tarzan books.

A NDY BRIGGS is a screenwriter, graphic novelist, and author. He has written for movie projects such as *Judge Dredd, Freddy vs. Jason,* and *Aquaman.* He also collaborated with *Spider-Man* creator Stan Lee and legendary producer Robert Evans on the screenplay for *Foreverman.* Briggs struck an eight-book deal with Oxford University Press for two series: Hero.com and Villain.net. His graphic novels include *Kong: King of Skull Island, Ritual,* and *Dinocorps.* He has recently rebooted the classic character Tarzan with his novels *Tarzan: The Greystoke Legacy* and *Tarzan: The Jungle Warrior.*

TARZAN EBOOKS

FROM OPEN ROAD MEDIA

Available wherever ebooks are sold

OPEN ROAD
INTEGRATED MEDIA

Open Road Integrated Media is a digital publisher and multimedia content company. Open Road creates connections between authors and their audiences by marketing its ebooks through a new proprietary online platform, which uses premium video content and social media.

Videos, Archival Documents, and New Releases

Sign up for the Open Road Media newsletter and get news delivered straight to your inbox.

Sign up now at
www.openroadmedia.com/newsletters

CPSIA information can be obtained at www.ICGtesting.com
Printed in the USA
BVOW080559150713

325698BV00002B/2/P